DEATH SHIP

MORTEM CYCLE
II

First Edition
Published by
Breaking Rules Publishing Europe, 2021.
This is a work of fiction. Similarities to real people, places,or
events are entirely coincidental.
Death House
Cover Design by
C. Marry Hultman
978-91-986841-4-8

THE MORTEM CYCLE

DEATH HOUSE
DEATH SHIP
UPCOMING TITLES
DEATH BEYOND
(Release Date 30th September 2021)

Who hath seen the Phantom Ship,
Her lordly rise and lowly dip,
Careering o'er the lonesome main,
No port shall know her keel again...
Ah, woe is in the awful sight,
The sailor finds there eternal night,
'Neath the waters he shall ever sleep,
And Ocean will the secret keep

— Albert Pinkham Ryder

CONTENT

FOREWORD

H.P. Lovecraft famously wrote in his essay Supernatural Horror in Literature that: "The oldest and strongest emotion of mankind is fear, and the oldest and strongest kind of fear is fear of the unknown." This is still very true, but as the knowledge of our world has expanded, the unknown has diminished. We, as humans, take pride in solving the mysteries of our world. There are a few murky parts still abound. One being the cold vastness of space, which happens to be the topic of our next anthology in this series, and the second being the depths of the sea.

Water covers 71 per cent of our planet and it may come as no surprise that we still do not know all the secrets hidden below the waves, and it is the same for all matter of bodies of water. From Nessie in Loch Ness, to the lost city of Atlantis, the mystery of the Mary Celeste, to the modern tragedy of Estonia. The fear of water has been a part of folklore since time immemorial. Mermaids, great floods threatening to wipe out mankind, dryads or fae luring young people into the lakes and so much more.

The horrors may come from any place, from hideous monsters below, to pirates attack on the surface to death from above. Staring out over the deep blue sea one realises that one stands at the mercy of nature and the elements.

Contained among these pages are stories of classic horror, fantasy, adventure and modern scares, but they all have one thing in common- that the main characters have nowhere to run, left to what horrors hide down below.

-C. Marry Hultman

ACROSS THE SEA

DAVID GREEN

"What are your orders, Captain?"

The voice drifted out of the gloom, a dead sound; flat, empty, like the air didn't want to carry it, wanted nothing to do with the men on *Aran's Bluff.*

"This darkness," Captain Lucy muttered to himself, scanning his surroundings from the tiller. He saw nothing but thick, black fog filling his deck, swallowing the souls on board. Couldn't even hear the waves that rocked the ship from side-to-side. "Ain't natural. Ain't natural at all."

He spat on the deck, an attempt to ward off evil. *Too late for that,* Lucy grimaced.

"Captain, please?"

Captain Lucy scowled, indecision wracking his

mind. They'd set off from Southampton for the New World forty days before, aiming for Cape Cod. An uneventful voyage, for the most part, until that morning. Instead of a crisp Spring mist and a biting breeze, black smoke drifted above the waves, the air dead and still. Stifling, too warm for the time of day and year. Now, sweat made Captain Lucy's skin slick; it dripped from his eyebrows, clung to his greying beard. He'd taken off his jacket as the fog gathered, grew thick. Unbuttoned his shirt, too. He'd sailed to the African sea on many occasions, down to the equator in the middle of summer. It felt like that now. It shouldn't.

The mist had developed into a thick, smothering gloom, revealing only the tiller ahead. Captain Lucy had ordered the lanterns lit. The mist swallowed their illumination. Around him, the *Aran's Bluff* creaked and groaned as they crawled without sight through the waves.

"Drop anchor," he commanded, his voice a hoarse whisper. Coughing, he raised his voice. "Drop anchor, I said!"

Echoes of feet slapping on the deck filled his ears as the crew complied. The anchor dropped, spinning until the entire length of rope unspooled. Just as Captain Lucy thought it wasn't enough, that the depths plunged too deep, he heard a yell of surprise as the anchor caught. Instead of lurching to a stop, the boat inched to a halt as it gained purchase, the ship ambling because of the low winds and still ocean.

"What now, Captain?" his first mate, O'Shay, called. His voice soft, as if he didn't want to disturb the mist.

"We wait," Lucy replied, turning to where he thought

his first mate stood. He couldn't see him. "This fog can't last forever. No point navigating where we can't see. We'll sit it out, get our bearings when it clears."

"Aye, Captain." Lucy thought O'Shay's voice carried a touch more confidence. The crew needed a show of strength, and he'd provide it for them by quashing his own doubts.

He started when he felt cold flesh in his hand. Jimmy the cabin boy stood at his side, starting up at him with wide eyes. The darkness reflected in them.

"Christ above, boy," Lucy grumbled, forcing a smile on his face, "almost gave me a heart attack."

The lad's tiny hand gripped his fingers.

"Sorry, Captain… I'm… it doesn't matter. Sorry." He didn't let go. Instead, his grip tightened. "What is this?"

A show of strength, Lucy thought, gritting his teeth. *That's what they need, this boy more than anyone.*

He glanced around, then smiled down at Jimmy, though the darkness almost swallowed his features from sight.

"Strange weather, no doubt about that," Lucy said with a wink, "but nothing your old captain ain't seen before. Odd things happen at sea, that's the beauty of it, eh? Wind shall soon pick up and take this gloom with it. Mark my words, lad. Now, until then, stay close. Fog's thick, so no wandering about the deck."

"Aye-aye, Captain."

Lucy started. At first, he thought the wind played tricks on his hearing, but then the air sat heavy and dead. Whispers, the voices of many, tugged at his ears, as if they spoke just to him. He couldn't make out the words, but their urgency made his hair bristle.

"You hear that, boy?" he muttered, staring down at Jimmy. The lad didn't need to answer; the alarm etched into his face made it clear he did.

"Who's out there?" a call rang out. O'Shay, the Captain thought, his force coming from the starboard side.

"What do you want?" another voice; high-pitched, on the verge of frenzy.

Lucy took a step towards Jimmy, laid a thick arm around the boy's thin shoulders. "Stay close to me, now, son."

The volume of the whispers increased; a hundred voices speaking at once. Faster and faster, over and over. Lucy gritted his teeth, jammed his eyes closed, and fought the urge to curl up on the deck, cover his head and weep.

His ears told him some of his men did just that. They screamed, wailed into the black night.

"No!" O'Shay yelled. "An accident! I swear, I didn't mean it. She fell, no fault of mine."

A blood-curdling wail ripped through the darkness, followed by a wet tear, like flesh being torn asunder. More screams answered, the voices belonging to Lucy's crew before a violent death snuffed them out. The Captain heard it all; that ripping of skin, the wet sound of organs, and blood gushing to the floor. He cast around, seeing nothing, hearing everything. Still the whispers continued, building in volume as the dying screams of his men built. Lucy let go of Jimmy, sank to his knees, head resting against the tiller. He banged his forehead against it, then again, harder each time. Pain exploded in his skull, fiery blood dripped into his eyebrows, but he didn't stop. And neither did the screams of the dying, the whispers surrounding him.

Until they did.

'Murderer.'

The voices turned into one by his side. Vision spinning, Lucy peered to his side. Jimmy the cabin boy watched him, his face twisted into a mocking grin, eyes pure of pure darkness.

'Murderer,' he spoke again, his voice echoing through the gloom.

"No one knows that," Lucy mumbled, stomach nauseous from his head wound, his throat dry. "Another life, a long time ago."

Jimmy cocked his head. But that smile widened. *'Murderer.'*

Smoke billowed from the boy's maw, enveloping Lucy. The Captain screamed as a thousand knives bit into his skin, and in his mind, the face of the man he killed appeared, the fellow he'd murdered for coin for ale. He'd stared into his eyes, ashamed, as the light left them.

Lucy screamed as his skin tore, and he remembered no more.

"How many more days to Cape Cod, Captain?" Edmund Towsey asked, closing his eyes and tilting his face toward the sun. The *Queen's Blessing* cut through the waves, the brisk wind welcome against the stifling day's heat, the two combining in a pleasant way.

"Each morning, the same damn question, man," Captain Reynolds grinned, his yellow teeth poking through his great black beard. "Yesterday, I said seven days. Today, it's six. What's the hurry? Don't you enjoy the ocean?"

"More than I realised," Towsey murmured, running his hand across the rail of the quarterdeck. He eyed Captain Reynolds; blue coat flowing behind him as he gripped the tiller, hair and beard streaming and looking every inch a pirate of legends. "You wouldn't give it up, would you?"

"Nay, man," the Captain boomed, shaking his shaggy head, "not for all the coin flowing across the seven seas. People such as you puzzle me."

Towsey smiled. "No offence, but I always think people like *you* are running from something. Me? I'm looking to sink my roots into the ground."

"And make a tidy profit on the side," Captain Reynolds laughed, slapping him on the shoulder. Towsey had braced himself against the lurch of the ship, but the man almost knocked him to the floor. "Lots of land in the New World, eh?"

Towsey regained his balance and shrugged. "Someone has to own it. I plan to build on it; houses, schools, businesses. It's what people need, and I've the means to provide it. The money made shall go into the properties after I take my wage, nothing more. Same way as I carry out my duty as a doctor, I only charge to cover my costs."

"You know, when you approached me about renting a cabin on this crossing, I wouldn't have believed you, but I've seen you look over the men. They appreciate it." The Captain pointed at Father Kelly, staring over the port rail, dressed all in black, as if the heat didn't affect him. The sweat pouring from his forehead abused that notion. "Reckon he's the only man aboard this ship more pious than you, and even then, reckon it's a close call."

Towsey studied the priest. The deckhands sang a jaunty shanty, their song ribald but pleasing. Father Kelly ignored it. In fact, he didn't appear to notice anything aboard the *Queen's Blessing.* Towsey had sought confession the day after leaving Plymouth, having not confessed for more than a week because of his impending departure and the need to have his affairs in order for the almost two-month journey. The Priest nodded his agreement, but only spoke to instruct Towsey to pray afterwards.

Father Kelly spoke to no one. He walked alone, kept his own counsel. Towsey had seen men like him before; men who'd done some great wrong, haunted by their past. But never a man of god. The Priest stared out to sea, clutching the Holy Book to his chest, and would stay there until nightfall.

"Kind words," Towsey replied, eyes still on Father Kelly, "but there's something about that man—"

"Captain!" A cry from the top of the mainmast. "Body in the water, off the starboard bow!"

"Crew, full-stop," Captain Reynolds roared. "Fish it out!"

Towsey raced in that direction as the crew worked to lower the sails and drop anchor. He glanced at Father Kelly as he ran by; the Priest hadn't moved, like the cry and sudden activity of the *Queen's Blessing* happened a thousand miles away and not on the deck he stood on.

"It's small, not moving," came a yell from the starboard bow rail, followed by a splash as a deckhand leaped into the ocean.

Towsey reached the spot as the crew threw ropes into the water for their mate to grasp. He gripped the rail in both hands, eyes narrowed as he watched the sailor—Bishop, he thought the man's name—reach the small body, wrapping an arm around it. *A child,* Towsey thought, making the sign of the cross. *Lord have mercy.*

"Got him," Bishop cried.

"Pull!" Fletcher, the first mate, instructed as Bishop grasped the ropes, the child in tow.

The men heaved, dragging their man and his quarry towards the *Queen's Blessing* and up over the rail. Bishop pushed the child first, a boy, and the men lowered him to the deck, his rescuer flopping onto the wooden planks beside him, gasping for breath.

"Fine work, men." Captain Reynolds had joined the throng and stood staring at the boy. "Is he alive?"

Towsey crouched, placing his ear by the boy's mouth. Air caressed his cheek. *It can't be,* he thought, eyes wide. "Aye, he breathes. Shallow, but steady."

He sat back on his haunches. He'd expected to attempt a futile resuscitation, fearing the boy long dead.

"Alive?" Fletcher exclaimed, then spat on the deck. "Where'd he come from? Ain't no ship that I can see. No land."

Good question, Towsey thought. He glanced over at Father Kelly, still staring out at the endless sea. Cape

Cod lay six days away, the shores of Ireland some forty-something behind.

A soft cough broke his concentration. Small, wet fingers grabbed his forearm.

"Where… where am I?"

Towsey surveyed the boy who looked back, brown eyes wide but flat, like the child had no emotion running through his body. No curiosity. No fear. It sent a chill through Towsey.

"The *Queen's Blessing,*" he replied. "We found you alone in the ocean. Where'd you come from? What's your name?"

The boy gave a steady blink. "I remember nothing. Just my name. Jimmy."

Towsey glanced at Captain Reynolds, who shrugged in reply.

"A miracle," the Captain smiled, hoisting the boy to his feet. "You're none worse for wear, and I need a cabin boy. You'll do fine. Lads, get us moving again."

Towsey watched the Captain and the child depart, heading to the Captain's cabin. Jimmy glanced back over his shoulder, expressionless as they locked eyes.

A touch on his arm almost made Towsey leap from his skin. Father Kelly stood by him, pointing over the bow. "Dark clouds on the horizon. Like a bruise in the blue sky."

Towsey turned to where the Priest pointed, surprise at hearing him speak and curiosity swelling within him. Sure enough, miles away, he saw them. A shadow growing in the distance.

"Just foul weather," Towsey murmured, smiling at

the Priest.

"Is that what your heart tells you?" Father Kelly replied. "Mine tells me there's trouble brewing."

Clutching the Holy Book, he strode below deck, whispering the Hail Mary. Towsey watched the black clouds on the horizon for a while, before gazing at the Captain's cabin. The rest of the crew had returned to their tasks, as if nothing untoward had happened, but Towsey knew better.

The boy, Jimmy, should have drowned.

"Captain Reynolds called it a miracle," he whispered, a stray chill biting at him. "I hope he's right."

Towsey sat at Captain Reynolds' table, enjoying a meal together as they often did. The crew ate below deck, but the Captain extended his welcome to the *Queen's Blessing's* guests, though Father Kelly had never joined them.

Until tonight.

Bible clutched to his chest, the Priest fixed his eyes on Jimmy, who'd settled into the role of cabin boy like he'd performed it all his life; refilling their plates and drinks without pause. Not that Father Kelly used either, Towsey noticed. His food and rum remained untouched.

"Well, the Priest won't say," Captain Reynolds slurred, holding his cup out for a refill. The man enjoyed his rum. Jimmy obliged, not with haste, but not slow, either. The Captain favoured him with a wink. "But I know there's more to your story about leaving England, Towsey. A man without adventure in his heart doesn't seek the New World unless he must. Priest's included. So say I, and you, too. Your words on seafaring men rang true… we all have something to run from. Yet here you are, on my vessel, crossing the vast ocean."

Towsey glanced at Father Kelly. He'd turned his eyes downward, staring through his meal. *Aye,* he thought, *the Captain's right there. About me. About the Priest, too. I've no doubt.* By his arm, Jimmy poured more rum. He felt the boy's eyes fixed on him, a feeling he'd had too often that night. Towsey took another bite of his cod, then laid the cutlery down and took a swig from his rum. It warmed his throat and belly, sent his thoughts loose a little. His tongue, too.

"I've lost something."

Towsey cut himself off, though an urge inside him pushed him to say more.

"You mean to find this… *something*… in the New World?" Captain Reynolds asked, spilled rum making his beard wet.

Towsey shook his head, eyes flicking to the Priest. He filled his mouth with rum once more. Only his nearest knew, and they numbered few, now. "My family. My wife and son."

The Captain raised his rum. Towsey's tone made the nature of their absence clear. "My condolences. Sickness?"

Memories flooded Towsey's mind, images from those hellish days and nights three years before, when Sarah and Thomas failed to arrive home. She'd taken their son to Plymouth for confession from their estate in the country and never returned. His community had searched high and low and found their mutilated corpses in a shallow grave on the outskirts of town days later. Towsey had wept for days; grief and a touch of madness assailing him, memories of his family's corpses haunting his waking hours and sleep.

Until his work pulled him back. His faith. Towsey glanced at Father Kelly. The red-headed man had grown pale. Dark rings stood out under his eyes, and his hands trembled on the bible he clutched.

"Not sickness." Towsey narrowed his eyes at the Priest. The man shook. "Murder."

Father Kelly lurched forward, knocking his untouched rum across the table. He shot to his feet, bible in hands.

"Excuse me. I feel… unwell."

Jimmy set to cleaning up the mess as Towsey watched the Priest hurry from the cabin, slamming the door behind him. He thought the man haunted before, but now it appeared those ghosts lurked on his shoulder.

"Curious fellow," Captain Reynolds mused, swilling his rum, then tossing it into his mouth. "Murder's a terrible business when dished out to those who don't deserve it. I'm sorry it befell you and yours, Towsey. Now, nature calls. Stay for one more drink, won't you? I'd hate to end the evening on this note. Bad omen."

The Captain pushed himself upright and staggered to his deck, intent on relieving himself over the rail. Towsey sat back, cup in hand, staring at the dark rum, his thoughts back to his family. He tried to live again in England, threw himself into his work, but he felt like he'd died when their bodies turned up. He needed the fresh start, even though heading to the New World felt like running away. But didn't he deserve a chance?

"There's so much sin aboard this ship."

He looked up. Jimmy stared at him from across the table. Ocean-tanned and wide eyed. Unblinking.

"What do you mean?" Towsey demanded, icy blood running through his veins.

"Everyone here has sinned."

He wanted to laugh. How could a child, a half-drowned boy not twelve hours before, know such things? His instincts forced his laughter down. They told Towsey that Jimmy told the truth.

"Even the Priest?"

A wide smile broke out across the boy's face. One that didn't reach his eyes.

"Oh, yes. God's man doesn't carry his forgiveness. Not for what he did." The boy cocked his head. "Everyone on this ship is a sinner. Everyone except you."

Towsey's hands curled into fists, his hackles rising at Jimmy's words.

"What did the Priest—"

The cabin's doors banged open, and the larger-than-life Captain Reynolds sauntered back in. "That's better. Nothing much in life beats an empty bladder! Boy, refill our drinks. We've demons to chase away."

The smile slid off Jimmy's face as it returned to his usual impassive, blank stare. The Captain hummed a shanty while Towsey downed his rum in one gulp. Thoughts on just what Father Kelly hid, and how the boy knew.

Nightmares assailed Towsey, dreams of Sarah and Thomas visiting him in his sleep. His wife watched him, her face a crimson mask of blood, silent and accusing. He heard the words, even though she didn't speak them: *'Where were you when we needed you, husband?'*

Thomas' face flickered between his and Jimmy's, the cabin boy wearing that wide grin that held no mirth, no joy. Behind them, a darkness lurked, like the shadow he and Father Kelly saw on the horizon that morning. Thick and black, it writhed behind his dead family. Waiting in the corner. Watching. Judging.

Towsey woke with a start, his bedclothes sodden with sweat, to find Jimmy watching him from the shadows, the whites of his eyes glinting in the candlelight. His mind made the link between where the boy stood and where the darkness loomed in his nightmare.

"What do you want, *boy*?" he growled, pushing himself upright and leaning his back against the wooden wall behind him.

Jimmy smiled, a twist of his lips at the way Towsey said *'boy.'*

"I know what the Priest did. I know what they all did." Towsey wanted to run. No, he wanted to dig his fingernails into his face and pull; tear his flesh from his face, scream. End it all in a river of blood. *Remember your faith, man,* he thought, breathing through his nose as his fingers fidgeted. *This is a test before you live your new life. God watches over you.* Jimmy cocked his head once more. "You think your god protects you here?"

"He protects me everywhere."

"Like how he stood by and watched your wife and child? How he did nothing as *he* mutilated them, cut pieces from them as they screamed for you and their salvation." The boy shook his head, tutting as he did. "That God?"

Towsey felt the heat leave his body. The room spun. He gripped the bedsheets, groaning as his past collided with his present. He'd asked himself the same questions, over and over. How could God do this to them? To him? What purpose did it serve? *A test,* Towsey repeated. *A test of my faith.*

"You said *he*." Towsey heard the words tumble from his mouth, like someone else spoke them. "You know who did this?"

Jimmy nodded. "I do, and now you understand that. Would you like me to tell you?"

A voice whispered in the back of Towsey's mind: *'No. It won't change anything.'* He gritted his teeth. He knew the answer, deep in his bones. He needed to hear it. "Yes."

"You're the only pious man on a ship filled with sinners, Edmund Towsey. Perhaps this will change that." The cabin boy turned to leave. As he opened the door, he paused and looked back. "Father Kelly murdered your family."

With a wide smile that didn't reach his eyes, the boy left, closing the door behind him. In his bed, Towsey wept, his faith beyond tested. He recalled his wife and child's broken bodies in that shallow grave, remembered as the mortician listed their many injuries and wounds, the things their murderer had done to them.

"I'll kill him," Towsey snarled, leaping from his bed. "God help me I shall."

His legs caught in his bedclothes and he crashed to the wooden floor, beating at it with his fists as he wept his soul empty.

Towsey emerged from below deck, murder in his heart, to discover a black morning.

A thick, heavy fog consumed the morning sky, limiting visibility to just a few feet ahead of him. The air felt dead, the crew silent. If he didn't hear the echoes of feet on the deck, he'd thought the ship deserted.

"Hello?" he called, casting about. He peered up to where the quarterdeck lay, but he couldn't see Captain Reynolds through the black mist.

Heat pummeled him. He loosened his shirt buttons, sweat sliding down his skin.

"They boys saw dark clouds on the horizon during the day, miles off still." Towsey lurched as he heard the Captain whispering by his side. The big man appeared smaller, subdued, his beard wet with vapour. "We awoke to this. Ain't natural. Between you and me, I reckon you should return below deck. Something's coming, my bones tell me it's so."

Towsey glanced to his side at the port rail. Through the swirling smoke, he saw Father Kelly standing there, staring out to sea.

"No, I don't think I shall," he replied, his voice low, almost a whisper. "What are your plans, Captain?"

The man sighed. "Not much we can do; there's no wind, but we're sailing blind. Full stop till this mist dissipates. If it ever does."

The Captain stomped off, his heavy steps ringing as he climbed the steps to the quarterdeck. Towsey swallowed and approached the port rail. Father Kelly didn't move when he drew near, didn't acknowledge his presence. The red-headed man's knuckles had turned white from his grip on the bible, his watery blue eyes, ringed with dark circles, fixed on the sea but viewing something else, a thousand miles away.

A push, Towsey thought, placing his hands on the rail. *That's all. No one will know in this darkness. No one will find him, but I need* him *to understand. As do I.*

"We're being judged," Father Kelly whispered, eyes still far away. "All of us, and we've been found wanting."

"A man of the cloth?" Towsey bit out, fingers flexing. How he hated this man, he told himself. How he'd crow when his body tumbled into the waves, how his heart would fill with joy as he watched him drown. So why did he hesitate? Why did he tell himself these things instead of feeling them? "If we're being judged, I'm certain you above all else shall be spared."

"I've sinned, Towsey."

"Lower the sails!" Captain Reynolds shouted.

Father Kelly turned that haunted stare on Towsey. Despite himself, pity surged from his gut. "Me, more than anyone else. A sickness twisted me for years."

Towsey felt something touch his hand, small fingers. He looked down to see Jimmy peering back up at him, holding his hand.

'*He killed your family.*' The boy's words rang in his head.

"Prepare to drop anchor!" Came the Captain's orders. If Towsey were to act, it had to be now. The *Queen's Blessing* still drifted forward; they'd lose Father Kelly's body in the water. A full-stop meant the crew could fish him out before he drowned.

Towsey took a step toward him, Jimmy's fingers tight as they gripped his hand.

"A sickness that made you kill women and children?" he snarled, though tears escaped his eyes.

"Yes." Father Kelly stared at him. That haunted look replaced with shame and regret.

'*Do it. Now. Give in. I can feel the urge inside you. Avenge them!*'

Time slowed. The smoky gloom appeared darker, blacker, just like the Priest's soul. The *Queen's Blessing* creaked and groaned as Towsey took another step closer, standing within arm's reach of Father Kelly.

"My family," Towsey gasped, "what you did to them…"

"I buried them, afterwards. I had to, when my senses returned. Please, you must believe me." Fat tears leaked from the man's eyes. "No doubt, I deserve to die. My end is near, I feel it. But know this, they were the last."

"Drop anchor!" Captain Reynolds screamed.

"That's supposed to make it right?" Towsey snapped. He just needed to let go of Jimmy's hand, reach out, and push. "You never—"

Father Kelly held up his hand, eyes darting back and

forth. "You hear that? The whispering? What are they saying?"

"Whispering?" Towsey spat. He heard nothing. Then it dawned on him; madness had broken the Priest's mind. Pity surged inside him again. "Perhaps you should go below deck."

The *Queen's Blessing* lurched as the anchor caught below the surface. Father Kelly continued to glance around him, eyes wild.

"Who's there?" Towsey heard the first-mate, Fletcher, cry. "Why are you saying those things?"

Other yells joined his. Cries of rage mixed with shame and regret as they questioned the voices Towsey couldn't hear.

Then Father Kelly screamed, a finger thrust out toward Jimmy.

Towsey turned, then fell to the deck, his hands still gripped by the cabin boy, who stared back with black eyes, his mouth opened wide, tongue lolling and black smoke leaked from his maw.

The boy's voice echoed in Towsey's mind. *'Kill him. Avenge your family before it's too late.'*

More screams joined Father Kelly's, who now leaned against the port rail, almost taunting Towsey with how easy it would be to dispose of him into the dark water. He heard a crash from the quarterdeck and saw Captain Reynolds stagger from the mist, his hands jammed against the side of his head, screaming at the top of his voice.

"Captain!" Towsey shouted, pulling his hand free of Jimmy. The smoke surrounding them, swallowing the ship, grew thicker. "Over here."

The sailor took a step before he wobbled, his screams rising in pitch. As Towsey watched, the Captain's body split down the middle, from crotch to skull, his organs spilling out to the deck as one leg tried to walk forward. His blood cascaded, landing on the wooden floor with a sickening splash.

'He robbed a woman, killing her husband in the struggle.'

Towsey vomited.

He heard a cry from the Main Mast, one that grew louder as Fletcher crashed to the deck, a bloody mess splattering as he landed.

'A cannibal.'

More screams, the sounds of the dead and dying, rang in Towsey's ears. He covered his ears to keep out the sound of tearing flesh, the splatter of blood and organs. By his side, Father Kelly did the same and all the while, the thing calling itself Jimmy stared at him with its black eyes, his voice ringing in Towsey's mind, telling him of the crew's sins.

Until silence reigned. Not even the waves dared make a sound.

'One left. You know his sin. Murderer, molester. Hiding behind the crook and lamb of your god.'

"Why do you want me to kill him?" Towsey screamed, glancing at the man. The Priest stared at him, then turned to the demon living inside a boy's body. "Why not end it all now?"

'Because you are pure, and you I cannot touch, and once the killing begins, I cannot leave. Let me help you,

believe me he deserves death.'

A bright white light bloomed in Towsey's vision. A gong rang inside his head and he fell backward but didn't hit the deck. Instead, he saw it all, every detail of the day Father Kelly murdered his wife and child. He witnessed the Priest stalk them, waylay them. He wept as he watched each thrust of the knife, every touch, heard every scream for mercy.

Towsey's head struck the deck, and his vision returned. Peering up, he locked eyes with Father Kelly. Rage surged, obliterating any pity he'd felt for the murderer.

"You bastard," Towsey snarled, baring his teeth. "I'll kill you, rip you to pieces with my hands for what you did to them!"

As he scrambled onto the deck, Father Kelly kicked him in the stomach, knocking him down again. He placed his foot on Towsey's chest, pinning him to the wooden planks. He dropped his bible, letting it fall beside his foot.

"No, I cannot allow that. You're a decent man, and my way into Heaven is blocked."

Jimmy screamed. The smoke swirled as Father Kelly turned and leaped over the port rail, dropping into the dark ocean below them. Towsey heard the splash, then silence. He pushed himself upright, sitting on the deck as he stared at Jimmy, the Priest's bible in his hands. For a minute, he watched the boy.

'Murderer. Molester of children. Blasphemer.'

Father Kelly made no sound as he drowned.

The wind picked up, thinning the black mist surrounding them. Towsey smelt salt on the air again, tasted moisture on his tongue, but still Jimmy watched him, his eyes returning to their usual brown, his face solemn.

"What now?" he asked the boy.

"I wait until you sin. Then your soul is mine, and I am free to move on."

Towsey glanced at the bible in his hands. "And if I never sin?"

"Then we're together until you die."

Nodding, Towsey pushed himself to his feet and stared over the port rail as the horizon revealed itself. Five days from Cape Cod, he could make it, or get close enough for another vessel to rescue him, but that meant giving the thing inside Jimmy more souls, more chances to move on. More chances to sin. He came close to killing Father Kelly. Too close.

Towsey thought of all the good he wanted to achieve in the New World, all the lives he could improve. Smiling, he realised he could do even better now.

He strode to the Quarterdeck and hoisted the anchor.

"What are you doing?" Jimmy asked, standing at the top of the stairs as the *Queen's Blessing* drifted once more.

Towsey checked the compass by the tiller and turned it so it aimed north. "Always wanted to see the frozen continent at the top of the earth before I died. Reckon I'll make that voyage now, if you don't mind."

Direction set, Towsey walked towards the Mizzen, ready to raise the sails. It would be tough getting the ship moving, but he could do it. He would do it to send this demon into the frozen wastelands, far away from where he could harm others.

Jimmy glared at him as he passed, hate burning in those brown eyes.

"Towsey," the demon growled. He paused, looked back. "One slip, and I'll be your end."

Edmund Towsey smiled, clutching the bible. "By that time, we'll be so far from civilisation it won't matter."

He got to work, raising the sails on the Mizzen. Someone would continue his work in the New World, and that comforted him. He thought of his wife and child, Sarah and Thomas, and redoubled his efforts. Towsey had one ultimate purpose, and he wouldn't fail

DEATH SHIP

BECALMED

TIM MENDEES

"How long are we going to be stuck here bobbing around like a blasted buoy, Captain? I'm expected back in Cornwall in three days. I stand to lose a lot of coin if I don't get my package to Betyls Cove in time for the auction."

Captain Jenkins sighed. His passenger, Rupert Lexington-Brown, had been moaning ever since they had set sail from Kingsport, MA. "What do you expect me to do, Sir? Climb up and blow in the blessed sails? It's not my fault there isn't any dratted wind."

Rupert puckered his mouth in indignation. "There's no need to be curt, Captain. I just want to know how long we will be stuck here. My employer will pay handsomely if you get me there in time."

"Look." Captain Jenkins rounded on his cantankerous passenger. "How the devil do you expect me to know? We are stuck here until the wind blows again and moaning at me about it isn't going to make it blow any quicker... neither is waving your employer's money around. Now, if you would excuse me..." Muttering under his breath, Captain Jenkins turned and stalked off down the deck, leaving Rupert with his mouth agape.

The sun was beginning to set, sinking towards the sea at a steady rate. Oranges and yellows danced on the top of the still waters. Affecting an air of nonchalance, Jenkins passed the confused deckhands and took the hatch to below decks. The crew were beyond confused. Most of them had served on the Cornish Queen for years, and never had it become becalmed before. Many thought it was an impossibility. The slightest gust should have been enough to keep the merchant ship's momentum going, so when it just stopped moving, the more superstitious amongst them whispered of curses. The Captain had to appear that nothing was wrong to avoid hysteria breaking out on deck. Though he was just as perplexed as his men.

Making his way to the crew-room, Jenkins scratched his mighty ginger beard in thought. Something was very odd about this entire situation. It had been plain sailing since they had weighed anchor, and they had been blessed with fine weather and calm seas... so there was no logical reason why they would appear to be so far off course. In the cramped room, away from the ears of the crew, his First and Second Mates stood puzzling over the map.

The First Mate, Wilkinson, puffed out his weather-beaten cheeks. "We should have seen other ships. There ain't no explanation other than we've drifted off the lane somehow."

"Impossible," his subordinate, Matthews, snorted. "We've made this run hundreds of times and didn't deviate in the slightest."

"Then 'ow the ruddy 'ell do you explain it? We should be able to see land to the north by now."

Matthews thought for a second, but no answer was forthcoming.

Captain Jenkins cleared his throat. "Gentlemen. Any bloody clue where we are yet?"

"I'm not sure we are off course, Captain." Matthews blustered. "We might not have made as good time as we thought."

"Cobblers!" Wilkinson barked. "I know this route like the back o' me hand, and I'm tellin' you, we're off course."

"I don't see it. I think we are where we should be, but stopped, that's all."

Captain Jenkins raised a hand for quiet. "I've always admired your optimism, Matthews, but we are definitely off course. I don't know how it's happened, but I need you to figure out where we are and get us back on course. So, if you could stop bloody squabbling for five minutes, I'd be most grateful."

Suitably chastised, Wilkinson and Matthews told the Captain everything they knew about their current situation, which, admittedly, wasn't much. They talked for fifteen minutes but made little headway. At the end of the day, they could discuss the maps as much as they liked. Without any wind, they weren't going anywhere.

"I don't understand it, Captain," Matthews confessed. "The Atlantic is one of the windiest places on earth. How can there be no wind?"

"Aye," Wilkinson added. "The sea's as flat as a table too... 'tain't natural."

"Now, now, Wilkinson." Captain Jenkins smiled. "You're starting to sound like some of the old-timers up on deck. It's just a freak occurrence, that's all."

"I 'ope you're right, sir," Wilkinson grumbled as he tapped his compass with his forefinger. "I really do."

Matthews rolled his eyes. Wilkinson was a fine sailor, but he was of the old school, curses and omens, and all that guff. Matthews followed the advances of science in Victorian society and scoffed at talk of the supernatural.

"In any case," Jenkins began. "Don't mention any of this to the crew. They are jittery enough as it is..."

As if to put an exclamation point on this statement, a commotion broke out above them, and one deckhand called down for the Captain.

"What now?" Jenkins scowled. "You two had better come with me. We may have to give them an extra rum ration to calm their nerves."

Following in silence, Matthews and Wilkinson did their best to appear unruffled as they climbed aloft. It was a bizarre sensation to step onto the deck and not feel a single gust of wind against their cheeks. The silence was unnerving. A ship was usually a cacophony of creaking timber, flapping sail, and clanking rigging. To hear nothing but the anxious mutterings of the crew sent waves of disquiet sloshing through their guts.

Jenkins paused by the topsail as he surveyed the scene. The crew were lining both sides of the boat, gazing and pointing into the water. Resuming his path, he tapped the quartermaster on the shoulder. "What's going on, Davey?"

Nearly jumping out of his skin, Davy turned and babbled. "Jellyfish, Cap'n, 'undreds of the buggers."

Leaning over the side, Jenkins peered into the water. Amongst strands of languidly drifting seaweed was a multitude of throbbing jellyfish. Each one was almost spherical, with thick fronds coiling around it. The way they moved was almost hypnotic. They seemed to be in synchronisation not only with each other but with the human heartbeat. And then there were the colours.

"Wilkinson?" Jenkins hissed quietly. "Have you ever seen anything like this?"

"Never. I've seen flutters before, but nowt like this."

"Matthews, you're our expert in exotic fauna. What type of jellyfish are these?"

"No idea, Captain. I've never seen anything like them, not even in books. Those colours..."

Jenkins nodded thoughtfully as he watched their luminous hides ripple through an astonishing spectrum of colours; some of which, he was certain, had no name. The sea around them glowed and pulsed, like it was somehow part of a gestalt entity. As he watched, time lost all meaning. He could feel his extremities start to feel lighter and his vision begin to blur. Snapping out of it, he pinched the bridge of his bulbous nose and turned away.

The crew seemed similarly transfixed. Each one had a slack jaw and glassy eyes. Turning to Matthews, he gave him a quick prod to the midriff and ordered, "get the men away from the sides. Give them something to do. Keep them busy, Mr Mate."

"Aye, sir." Matthews gabbled, returning to reality. A moment later, he was strutting along the deck, barking orders. It never ceased to impress Jenkins how Matthews could find jobs when there were none. He could have rivalled the Devil himself when it came to making work for idle hands.

"Captain," Wilkinson said in dire tones, gazing out to sea.

"Hmm?"

"There's a fog rolling in, look."

Captain Jenkins turned and stared in confusion. There had been nothing to see but a flat horizon only moments before. Now there was an impenetrable miasma heading in their direction. "What the hell?"

"It's not right, sir. There's somethin' evil about it."

Jenkins grabbed Wilkinson by the shoulders. "Keep your damn voice down and get a ruddy grip! It's odd, I grant you that, but there's nothing evil about it... It's just a fog."

"Yes, sir... Sorry, sir. It's those damn jellies. They've got me spooked, sir. I feel like they're watchin' me."

"I know, Wilkinson." Jenkins smiled as he let go of his sleeves. "They are enough to give any sailor the willies but don't let your imagination run riot. They are just jellyfish, albeit odd ones, they can't harm us if we don't go in the water..."

"Captain!" a voice cried out from the aft of the ship. It was Matthews.

"What now?" Jenkins spat as he looked down at some commotion on deck. "Come on, Wilkinson, you too, Davy."

A group of men, including Matthews, struggled to get a large rigger off of Rupert. He was roaring and spitting like some wild beast. His shovel-like hands were clamped firmly around Rupert's neck, attempting to throttle the life out of him.

"What the hell is going on, Matthews?" Jenkins demanded as he joined the struggle.

"He was staring at the jellyfish, sir. I grabbed him by the shoulder, and he pushed me on my arse!" Matthews was outraged. "Next thing I know, he's punched Mr Lexington-Brown in the nose and is trying to kill him."

Finally managing to release the crewman's grip and bending one arm behind his back, Jenkins shouted over at Davy. "Quartermaster, get him below decks!"

"Aye, sir!"

A moment later, the crazed sailor was being bundled off by Davy and two stout crewmen. Taking a deep breath as he smoothed out his jacket, Jenkins quizzed Matthews further. "Did he say anything, or give any indication as to why he would want to hurt Mr Lexington-Brown?" Aside from the obvious, he thought, but didn't say.

"No, sir. He was babbling, but it was just gibberish." Matthews grunted as he and Wilkinson helped the battered antique dealer to his feet. "If I was a religious man,

Captain, I'd say he was speaking in tongues."

"Well?" Jenkins turned on Rupert. "Any idea what that was all about?" He passed him a handkerchief, which quickly turned from white to red.

"No... nothing. I'd never even spoken to the ruffian before. I must say, Captain, this is an outrage! What kind of ship are you running here? I have a good mind to report you when we get home."

Jenkins bit his lip and balled his fists. Counting to ten, he tried to resist the urge to add to the damage already done to the man's beak. "Do as you see fit, Mr Lexington-Brown, but let me remind you that the reason you are travelling on a merchant ship is that you wanted to avoid any unwanted questions about your cargo by those fine, upstanding gentlemen in customs. I can't imagine that you would like me to tell them about the bundles of tobacco you may have used to pack your antiques with, would you?"

Rupert's skin turned as red as the blood trickling from his nostrils. "I... I..."

Checkmate. Jenkins relaxed his fists and smirked. "I thought not."

"Sir," Wilkinson interjected. "The fog, sir. It's all around us now."

"Indeed, I can feel it clawing at my bones... Matthews, keep the crew active and break out the rum ration. Wilkinson, you come with me, let's see what our would-be murderer has to say for himself."

The sickly yellow glow from the dim lamplight illuminating the cabin made shadows dance around Captain Jenkins and Wilkinson as they looked down at the stricken crewman sitting on his bunk. He looked dazed and confused. His body trembled, and his jaw hung slack.

"Has he said anything, Davy?" The Captain asked as he peered into the sailor's bloodshot eyes.

"No, sir. He's just sat there, watchin' the shadows. If ye ask me, he's got a touch of the sun, sir."

"Very good, Davy. You can leave us, what's the chap's name, Patrick something?"

"Collins, sir. Pat Collins. Joined us on the last run and never been a problem."

As Davy turned and walked in the direction of the lower deck hatch, Captain Jenkins waved his hand in front of Pat's eyes. Nothing. Not a flicker. "Patrick? Can you hear me?"

Wilkinson snapped his fingers close to the man's left ear. Jenkins flinched, but Pat didn't. "It's no good, Cap'n. He's away with the blasted faeries."

"Pat." Jenkins continued, ignoring his first mate. "Why did you attack Mr Lexington-Brown? Was it something to do with the jellyfish?"

Wilkinson cocked an eyebrow and looked at the Captain like he had just dropped off the moon. "Sir?"

"Hush, Wilkinson..."

Slowly, Pat's jaw started to move. "They... want."

"They?" The Captain pressed. "The jellyfish? What do they want Pat?"

"Captain!" Davy's voice echoed from down the corridor.

"What now?" Jenkins sighed. "Keep an eye on Pat,

I'll be right back."

"Aye, sir."

Navigating the crew's personal effects, Jenkins hurried out into the narrow corridor and headed in the direction of the stern. Davy was crouched by the hatch to the lower deck with a look of horror on his face.

"What is it, Quartermaster?"

"Jellies... look. They've got into the bilge water, Captain!"

"What?" Jenkins ushered Davy out of the way and peered into the foot of stagnant water that had collected at the bottom of the ship. The bilge of the ship was glowing like a Lewis Carrol fever dream. The water was full of the bulbous jellyfish, their gelatinous bodies huddled together, giving the bilge an organic look. "By, Christ. Have you ever seen the like?"

"I ain't Sir. And I pray, I never did... It's not natural, Captain. This is Devil's work."

Looking around in the dusty corners of the corridor, Jenkins located a bent nail and picked it up. He raised his hand slowly, took aim, and tossed it at one of the larger specimens. "Bloody Hell!" He and Davy cried in unison as several inky black eyes popped open on the creature's hide. It started to vibrate angrily, thrashing its fronds out of the water. The disturbance awoke the adjacent jellies, then the ones adjacent to them. Soon, every jellyfish in the bilge was staring up at them with hateful little eyes."

"Look out, Captain!" Wilkinson screamed from down the corridor. They had been so distracted by the unnatural creatures that they hadn't seen Pat stumble out into the corridor and start to run in their direction.

"C' goka ahf' c' ah, shoggoth nafl'fhtagn!" Pat was screaming and roaring, his eyes rolled back in his skull, his facial muscles taut and skin strained. He was running full pelt for the open hatch.

Davy pushed Captain Jenkins aside and launched himself in a rugby tackle at Pat. Connecting with his midriff, both men were sent tumbling by the momentum. Pat went headfirst into the bilge while Davy's legs dangled through the aperture. Jenkins grabbed Davy by his belt as Patrick's screams and a hideous gurgling sound echoed through the lower deck.

Wilkinson joined Jenkins in helping Davy out of the hatch. "Sorry, sir. He took me by surprise. Come at me like an angry ox, he did!"

Davy was almost out of danger when a long frond snapped around his ankle with a whip-like crack. He bellowed in agony as the monstrous jellyfish administered its sting. Jenkins let go of the agonised quartermaster as his skin around the frond began to ripple and jellify. His clothes melted away as the sting spread.

"Back! Let go, man!" Jenkins ordered as he leapt over Davy's body and grabbed Wilkinson by the shoulder. Drawing his Colt Navy revolver, he levelled it at Davy's head. The poor man was being dissolved into a gelatinous mass that throbbed and pulsed with the same colours as the jellyfish. "I'm sorry, Davy." He said as he squeezed the trigger.

Bang!

Davy's head popped like a grape.

Jenkins and Wilkinson were horrified to see that the change continued to happen to Davy's body. In seconds, he had been completely engulfed. To make matters worse, another amorphous mass was rising out of the hole behind him. It was Pat, presumably. The two men had been utterly subsumed and were now little more than enormous jellyfish-like creatures.

Backing away slowly so as not to agitate the twin monstrosities, Jenkins and Wilkinson edged towards the deck hatch. The abominations throbbed, vibrated, and tasted the air with their rope-like tendrils, seemingly adjusting to their new forms. The terrified mariners were nearly at the hatch when it suddenly swung open, and Matthews bellowed below...

"Captain, come quick!"

Alerted by the noise, hundreds of hideous eyes snapped open on the skin of the creatures.

"Run!" Jenkins screamed.

Tekeli-li!

The creatures piped frenziedly as they started to surge with alarming rapidity down the narrow walkway. Wilkinson practically flew up the ladder and knocked Matthews flying. Turning on his heels, he grabbed the Captain by the shoulders and yanked him the last foot out of the hatch. Landing in a heap, the frantic mate screamed at Matthews to close the hatch.

Startled and confused, Matthews grabbed the hatch and looked down just as a hideous bulk slammed into the ladder. A high-pitched yelp escaped his throat as he slammed the hatch down as hard as he could.

"Quickly," Jenkins panted as he scrambled to his feet. "We need to weigh it down."

Matthews crouched on the hatch as the creature

slammed it from below. It was possessed with such strength that it nearly launched him up to the topsail yardarm. "Hurry!" He screamed as he tried to put as much weight as possible on the hatch.

Jenkins and Wilkinson commenced piling heavy sacks, coils of rope, and anything else they could find on the hatch. Matthews joined them as the creature continued to thump the hatch from below. After a while, the banging stopped, and the creatures could be heard slurping their way back down the corridor.

"Good job." Wilkinson panted.

"What in God's name was that thing?" Matthews asked, his eyes wide with terror.

"That, Mr Mate, was Quartermaster Davy," Jenkins said grimly. "Now, what did you call for?"

In all the excitement Matthews had almost forgotten. "It's the crew, Sir. Some of them are jumping overboard."

"Captain, look." Wilkinson pointed down towards the aft. The fog was so thick that they couldn't see six feet in front of them. It coiled and twisted like it was alive. Splotches of rippling colour heightened the effect. "I think more of those things have got on deck."

Matthews gibbered and snivelled as he peered over the side of the ship. Several of the globular creatures were slithering up the side of the vessel like slugs.

"It's the ones that have eaten." The Captain surmised.

"What do they want?" Matthews sobbed. "Why us?"

It was then that the pieces clicked together in Jenkins' mind. "We need to find Rupert Lexington-Brown, quickly." Crouching low against the side of the ship, he crept into the fog. Wilkinson followed and dragged the near-hysterical Matthews with him. As they crossed the deck to the mainmast, one of the glowing blobs plopped onto the deck behind them. Matthews turned and screamed. In a flash, the creature had charged forwards and engulfed him.

"Run!" Wilkinson screamed and pushed Jenkins ahead of him. The two men charged blindly into the fog as the creature digested its meal. The fog was so thick that they quickly became disorientated. Screams filled the night as the crew were hunted down and absorbed one-by-one. Jenkins pushed Wilkinson out of the way just as a body slammed into the deck from above. The poor devil had tried to climb to safety but slipped and tumbled to his doom. Jenkins despaired. It was Rupert Lexington-Brown.

"Now what?" Wilkinson asked as he looked around frantically for a place to hide.

"It must be his cargo. That special item he had to get home so damn quick."

"That's madness, Sir, what would a bunch of jelly monsters want with some old antique?"

"I don't know, but remember what Pat said, 'They want.'"

"Where is it?"

"In my cabin, come on!" Giving every glowing patch of fog as wide a birth as possible, the two men scurried towards the stern, nearly running straight into the mizzen mast. They were nearly at the cabin door when the deck behind them erupted in a shower of splintered timber.

Tekeli-li!

"Christ, it's Davey! Run, Wilkinson!"

Wilkinson, knocked off balance by the twisting planks, stumbled and crashed into the side of the ship. Jenkins howled in anguish as his best friend and second-in-command was lashed by a writhing pseudopod and dragged screaming into the quivering abomination that had once been Davy.

With tears stinging his eyes, Jenkins crashed into his cabin and slammed the door. Locking the bolts at the top and bottom, he shuffled back from the door, brandishing his pistol in his trembling hand. Muttering prayers and spitting oaths, Captain Jenkins crossed his cabin and dragged the small chest out from under his bed.

Placing the barrel of his gun close to the lock, he fired once and gained entry. Frantically, he pulled out packet after packet of Virginian tobacco and tossed it behind him. As he dug into the chest, the creature slammed against the door. Its weight, newly doubled, would make quick work of the flimsy locks... Jenkins was running out of time. Eventually, his hand landed on an object wrapped in an oilskin. Dragging it out, he started to unwrap it.

Rupert's treasure appeared to be a strange diadem fashioned from a strange kind of alloy. It glittered in an almost lemon hue. The design was unlike anything he had ever seen before. The curves and embellishments resembled some bizarre deep-sea coral. Mesmerised by its grotesque beauty, Jenkins ran his hand over the metal.

As soon as his skin made contact, the cabin melted away around him, and he was suddenly somewhere else...

Jenkins was seeing through the eyes of a heavy-set man in a long black coat. Next to him, and similarly dressed, was another man who he instantly recognised... it was Rupert Lexington-Brown.

"I think it's safe if we are jolly quiet." Rupert grinned.

Rain was lashing down on the furtive duo in thick rods as they lurked outside what looked like a masonic hall. Gazing up at the front of the building, Jenkins could make out the words 'Esoteric Order of Dagon' painted under an ichthyic eye design.

"Come on, man." Rupert insisted. "Don't just stand there where every gill-breather in Innsmouth can see you."

This was beyond frustrating for Jenkins. He could see and feel as though he was really there but couldn't influence the events. It was even more bizarre when the body he inhabited spoke. "Coming... go around the side, I pre-forced the basement window at the rear."

The two men slipped around the rear of the white-washed building, picking their way over weed-tangled flagstones that stuck out of the earth at jaunty angles. They jimmied the basement with ease and slipped into a dank basement. Rupert struck a match and lit a candle-stub that he brought out of his inside pocket.

"Where is it?" Rupert asked.

"The diadem is kept in that cupboard at the back. I

saw the priest put it in there when I was casing the joint."

"Good work, Smith." Rupert purred as he made his way across the cellar and opened the cupboard doors. "I knew you were the chap for the job. We will be rich men once we get this trinket back home." Reaching inside, he brought out the oil-skin parcel, checked its contents, then pocketed it. "That's it, come on."

Rupert pushed in front of his accomplice and climbed out of the window. Smith made it half-way out when his leg was grabbed by two webbed hands. Rupert caught a glimpse at the frog-like face of Smith's attacker through the window, screamed, and ran into the night...

Shaking his head as the cabin reappeared around him, Jenkins dropped the diadem. "What the hell was that?"

Crash!

A chunk of the cabin door flew past his head and clattered into the wall. A snaking pseudopod slithered through the gap and into the cabin. Jenkins grabbed the diadem and scrambled backwards on his haunches as it thrashed around the cabin.

"Here, take it," Jenkins cried, holding out the diadem. It was no good. The creature couldn't understand that he was trying to return the sacred object. With no other option available to him, Jenkins placed the hateful object onto his cranium.

Instantly, the creature, which he now knew to be a Shoggoth, stopped and withdrew its appendage.

'Return what is ours,' an insidious voice hissed into

his brain. 'Return it, and you will be spared.'

"Back away from the door!" Jenkins demanded.

The Shoggoth complied. Jenkins' mind was filled with information. The diadem belonged to a pre-Adamite race known as Deep Ones that served a deity known as Dagon. They used it to control a servitor species known as Shoggoths. After Rupert had stolen it, a flutter of pro-to-Shoggoths set out from the breeding grounds around Kingsport and Innsmouth in hot pursuit.

"Back in the water, all of you."

Again, the Shoggoths complied, one-by-one, they splashed into the water, leaving the few surviving sailors staring at their Captain in bewilderment. Once they had all gone back into the water, Jenkins gave them one last order before tossing the diadem into the water.

"Take it and return to where you came from."

Seconds after the diadem hit the water and was grabbed by one of the creatures, they all sank into the depths and vanished. Jenkins collapsed to the deck, exhaling for the first time in what felt like hours. Two of the surviving crew rushed to his aid, one of them calling out, "look, the fog's clearing!"

Handing Jenkins a flask of rum, one of the battered and bruised sailors hauled him to his feet. "I don't know what ye jus' did, sir... but I reckon ye jus' saved our necks."

Jenkins took a gulp of rum and watched the fog disperse as swiftly as it had appeared.

Then the wind began to blow...

THE BELL IN THE SEA

C. MARRY HULTMAN

"It looks like a human child," the simian Buhlo said and scratched the black fur on his chin.

"A Gaet by the looks of it," Carain, the first mate replied.

Both of them were peering over the railing, looking at the tiny figure dressed in a tattered outfit, face down atop a door.

"Is it alive?" Sona the Whisperer inquired. Her steel gray eyes squinting.

"It looks like it is breathing, but it difficult to tell from here," Carain replied.

"What do we do?" Buhlo asked and cast a glance over his shoulder, worried that the captain might be near.

"Take it to my quarters," Carain also turned around and waved the albino twins Hampus and Ward over.

They were two weeks out of Atrista, slovenly sailing on Grand Theio, the southern sea when they came across the lifeless gaet barely alive on the makeshift raft. Carain watched the crew move the child from his perch on the quarterdeck. The sun mercilessly beating down on his tanned skin, while his gray hair, intricately tied in a braid moved in the slight breeze. He had removed the heavy jacket of his uniform to allow the wind to caress his thin frame through his white linen shirt. Raised on the water, like all greì - the sea elves - he felt one with the element. Knew its every movement and sensed changes is mood as an old companion, but of late he yearned for solid ground. He leaned back and tried to listen to the water like one listen to an old friend. Something carried on the wind. The sound of some distant ringing, dull, yet at the same time cutting through the wind.

The ship Vereem carried a motley crew of sailors. Simians, cattons and various other scoundrels. Not the assortment of tip top bodies Carain would have signed on, but the infamous Captain Black Dok had a reputation for gathering the worst scum around. The greì had always been impressed by the man's ability to get the best out of each and every individual. He possessed an uncanny knack for finding the talent of a crew member and using it for his own personal gain. Never becoming attached to them on a personal level, Black Dok wept not a tear for the expendable lives lost under his command,

and there were always deaths on the Vereem. They were pirates. Carain felt no pride in his occupation and if he had the choice he might have signed on to another vessel, but the brand on his right cheek guaranteed no one would want his services.

Black Dok had rescued him from a fate worth than death for a greì. Drunk and dejected in the dirty alleyways of Atrista. Wanted by none. The notorious captain knew not to pass on a sea elf, someone who could read the ocean. So, Carain owed Black Dok his life and the horrible captain let him know this every time he stepped foot on the creaking boards of the ship.

All in all, they did get along well enough. At least was well as a greì bound by duty could be. Carain avoided ruffling any feathers, both figuratively and literally. Some had paid a steep price speaking up against Black Dok. If Carain never saw another limp body fished from the depths after having their skull crushed against the keel it would be too soon.

"An ill wind is brewing," Sona the Whisperer had joined him.

"True," Carain replied and turned back to the dark waters. "Not quite a storm, but not a stern breeze either."

"I cannot quite put my finger on it," Sona tilted her head to listen to the wind. Her slender fingers, heavy with silver rings clutching her Wind Talker staff.

Like him she was greì, from a different island, but enough alike in appearance and culture that they had an instant report. How Black Dok had recruited her he dared not ask, but everyone had a price on the Vereem.

She shuddered for a moment, as if catching a chill, not surprising as her thin dress billowed around her like the sails of the three masts. Sona lost her balance and Carain darted forward to catch her, but she managed to recover before hitting the deck slick from ocean spray.

"What is it, Sona?" He knelt beside her as she tried to find her bearings.

She still clutched her staff with a desperate grip. "There is something out there Carain," she panted. Gray locks covering her face. "Something I have never felt before. Like an evil lying in wait. A spider ready to pounce on the helpless insect tangled in its web. Interwoven with that human child."

"Wyle," Carain snapped his fingers and a catton, covered in orange fur slid down from the crow's nest with lightning speed.

"How can I help, Carain?" the feline figure said as she landed deftly on the deck in front of him.

"The Whisperer needs assistance," Carain said. "I would like you to make sure she gets settled."

Wyle blinked slowly and her pointed ears twitched at the notion of having to do more work than otherwise needed, but Carain stood above her on the hierarchal ladder and she needed to obey. The close relationship between the captain and his second made little room to doubt that any insubordination would be severely dealt with. No matter what.

"I will make certain she is safe, Sir," Wyle almost spat the last word. "Why do you not scale the mast and keep a lookout in my stead?"

Carain smiled and let out a chuckle. "You would love to see me fall and break my neck."

The catton smiled as she glanced back at him while carrying the limp Sona in her arms.

As the two figures vanished, he heard the unmistakable disharmonious rhythm of a webbed foot and peg-leg striking the wood behind him. Quickly he tucked his shirt into his pants and patted down any stray hairs that might have escaped the braid.

He turned and looked down at Captain Black Dok, who tapped his foot with an annoyed scowl on his feathered face. In a vain attempt to mimic the smacking of soft lips his bill, complete with piercings, clicked together. The familiar sign that someone might meet their demise on this day.

"What is this I hear of a gaet child?" Black Dok crossed his arms.

"It would appear that the storm from last night washed up something," Carain took a step back and looked down on his captain.

"Storm?" Since Dok did not have eyebrows it could be difficult to read his expression. It made him extremely unpredictable.

The previous night Carain had woken from a dead sleep by the sound of knocking on his window. He rolled out of his cot and padded over to the window to look out only to be met by large balls of hail bouncing off the glass. The water moved in dark angry waves splashing the side where his quarters lay, threatening to break the thin barrier between him and nature. As he stared out at the untamed rolling beyond the window, he thought he could hear the sound of a bell in the distance, followed by a loud shrieking wail.

He decided that it must be the late night, the creaking from the ship and the hard weather playing tricks on him. Sailors would go mad for less. The constant sounds of a ship at sea.

He had decided to step out on the deck, uncertain sleep would find him again. The wind howled as he stepped onto the deck slick with water. The ship moved violently from side to side and the crew had lowered the sails in an effort to avoid capsizing. Carain grabbed the railing to avoid slipping and getting washed out one of the ports.

Only the twins, Hampus and Ward were still outside. Both of the pale, ginger, men clutching a mast, as rain and hail beat at them and the wind attempted to rip from safety.

Suddenly the sky exploded as lightning tore through the sky with a large crack and a tall wave crashed over the deck and at the same time the ringing sound grew louder. Almost closer than before once again followed be the shrieking wail. It sounded angst-ridden, like mournful call for companionship. Several other voices chimed in creating a choir of pain.

"She sensed something out there. Something dangerous." Carain pointed to the horizon.

"Something more dangerous than Black Dok himself?" The pirate squawked.

"Indeed, Sir," Carain agreed and tried to join into

the mirth. "I do believe it is wise to stay vigilant. Maybe the twins patrolling the deck this eve."

"I am sure the Whisperer only sensed the remnants of the storm," Dok stood on the toes of his one foot to peer over the railing. "What she needs to be listening for is another ship. I am itching for a fight, and for loot."

"The men are getting restless Sir," Carain placed his hands on his back. "No doubt feeling the same."

"Then head south, first mate," Dok walked past Carain and patted him firmly on his stomach.

"But we have not ventured this far before Captain," Carain felt a worried sensation in his gut. They had no charts over the most southern regions of Grand Theio.

"Why the concern, Carain?" Dok stopped but did not turn to look at him. "Are you not greì? Can you not sense the water? Feel her movement, through the hull of this great ship? Are you not one with her, call her mistress, lover, mother, father, sister or brother?"

Carain shuddered at the words. Most people thought of Black Dok as a dim-witted sailor, more evil than calculating, but they had not seen his true nature.

According to pirate lore, Black Dok had been a farmer in another life, with a wife and younglings. He had fallen on hard times, and unable to pay his debts or afford to grow new crops. Then subsequently ousted by the landowner. He snapped one night, killed his family, burned down the farm and traveled to the manor of his debtor. Climbing through a window Dok snuck into the man's bedroom and summarily slit his throat with a sickle, then proceeded to do the same to the rest of the household. That same sickle now hung from his weathered leather belt. Around his throat a necklace made from the teeth of fallen enemies. Another statement of jealousy.

"We head into the unknown," Dok continued without expecting an answer. "The gods bestow fortune on those who tempt the fates."

"So, the child keeps rambling about some ship it was on," Sona turned to Carain, Buhlo and Dok who were standing next to the first mate's cot.

They established that they were dealing with a human girl. Her black hair and dark skin indicating that she must be from the southern region of Gaetland. Sona, the only one aboard The Vereem with any healing skills, since Dok had killed their last medic, had cared for her, but quickly called for the rest as soon as the child stirred.

"Has she said anything more specific?" Carain asked as the girl moaned.

"No, she just repeats the words Nord and bell," Sona replied.

"The Nord is a vessel that traffics these parts," Dok had a wealth of knowledge inside his feathery head. At least as it pertained to maritime facts. "A transport ship if I am not mistaken."

"Where am I?" The soft, yet groggy voice of the child cut through Carain's eyeroll.

She attempted to scoot backwards on the cot, but the awkwardness of the piece of furniture swung wildly and threatened to send her sprawling to the floor. Her reaction to seeing two grei, a simian and a duck staring at her did not surprise any of them.

"Take it easy child," Sona said in a soothing voice.

The girl's eyes were wide open, as if she might be searching for something, or expecting someone to attack her. "Where is everyone else? Mother? Father? The rest of them?"

"Please take it easy, my dear." Sona attempted to calm her down. Carain noticed the subtle purple glow at her fingertips.

The tension in the girl's face mellowed, she seemed to relax, and her eyes took on a dreamy quality, as if they were staring far off in the distance. Sona looked at Carain and nodded. He approached the cot and placed a hand on the girl's knee.

"Tell us child," he paused, realizing he did not know her name. "How come we find you floating alone out here in the middle of uncharted waters?" He also realized he did not know how to speak to children.

The girl, relaxing even more, tried to move towards him. Mesmerized by his almond shaped gray eyes and similar dark complexion. She looked to be about twelve, but Carain, who aged slower than humans struggled to assess this.

"I traveled with my mother and father, Chael and Escaïn Folg and we were sailing with a gift to an island close to our lands."

"Lord and Lady Folg?" Dok, who had turned to leave, suddenly paused.

"You know them Captain?" Buhlo asked.

"They are high nobles in the outer isles," Dok rubbed his hands together.

"Do you know what happened to them?" The girl

became excited.

"No," Dok padded towards her, the lust for treasure in his yellow eyes. "Tell me of this gift your parents were traveling with, my dear."

"I only saw it as our servants loaded it into the cargo. A large bell. Like for a temple tower. One that calls us to prayer."

"A gold bell?" Dok began foaming at the mouth.

"Maybe," the captain's visage began rattling the girl.

"Captain?" Carain said.

Dok took a deep breath, then grabbed Carain by the collar and dragged the bent shape off towards the door.

"If the Folgs brought a large bell to one of the other kingdoms to the south, then they probably brought other valuables as well. The outer islands have been at war for decades and this seems like a peace offering to me. I can hear the clink of gold, Carain."

Whenever Black Dok smiled his toothless grin, an unnatural expression for one of his race, it sent shivers up and down Carain's spine.

"What of the ship?" Carain whispered. "If she was floating by herself it must surely have sunk during the storm."

Dok smacked his bill together and held up a finger to the first mate.

"My dear," his words sickly sweet. "What happened to the ship? What happened to The Nord?"

The girl motioned for Sona to help her out of the cot. "I do not know."

"Pardon?" Dok stifled his instant rage. "Come

again?"

"All I remember is the sound of that bell as we moved up and down the water." She replied and stared beyond the assembled figures, as if in a trance. "They never secured the clapper inside. It swung back and forth as the waves crashed against the sides. As soon as we left home the sound of the bell began. Then at night as I lay in my bed, I thought I heard something answer it. Something out there in the depths. The further out to sea we ventured the closer that something felt. We could hear it wail in the middle of the night. Then the storm came."

"The storm that sunk The Nord?" Carain asked.

"The ship did not sink," the girl replied and came out of her fugue state to look at the first mate. "Mother and Father told me to hide in my cabin in order to be safe. I hid under my blanket when the thunder and heavy rain came down around us. I thought I could hear more cries and something moving about in my room. I shut my eyes so tight and wrapped the blanket around me until I fell asleep."

Carain, Black Dok and Sona stood on the quarter deck and gazed out over the calm waters, contemplating what they had just heard.

"That is some story," Carain said. "Waking up to find the entire ship abandoned. Do you believe her?"

"There is no indication that she is lying," Sona replied. "Not as far as I can sense."

"So, she wakes up after the storm, found The Nord completely devoid of life only to grab a door to use as a raft. Sounds unlikely."

"What would you do?" Bulho chimed in as he padded up from the main deck. "The girl's a kid, I think. I can never quite tell with her kind. She told us the life rafts were gone. She thought everyone else left so she tried to do the same. She would not be able to commandeer a ship herself."

"Is it not queer that the ship showed no signs of life?" Carain continued.

"Who is to say," the simian came to lean on the railing. "They probably forgot her in the panic of fearing the ship would sink."

"The Nord is still out there," Black Dok's wretched voice cut in. "I want her. I want the bell and whatever treasure they were carrying. Before the crew returns, which they might."

"You want us to look for an abandoned ship out here? We do not even know where to head."

"That is what she is for," Dok pointed to Sona, who closed her eyes and listened.

"If they have returned then we return the child in exchange for a tidy reward, unless we attack." Dok winked at Carain.

"We should turn the ship around," Sona interrupted. "The Nord is still out there. I can hear the bell on the breeze and the creaking of the timbers from the hull."

"Excellent," Dok lifted his cap and smoothed back the feathers on his head. "Assemble the crew. We need to get there, double time."

The had begun to set when The Nord came into view. Bobbing along in a leisurely fashion. Sails completely still and tranquil as they approached. No light and no signs of life in the slightest.

"I need The Whisperer, Buhlo, Wyle, the pale twins and you Carain to join me aboard," Dok said.

He never left anything to chance. Never trusted anyone but himself to get a job done. Especially as it pertained to plunder.

"I think we should take the girl as well," Carain replied as the entering hooks flew over the railing and attached to the other vessel. "She is familiar with the ship and could prove valuable."

"I like the way you think Carain," Dok tapped his bill with amusement. "If the Folgs return we have her as our excuse to aboard."

An eerie sensation wafted at the crew as they placed their feet on the deck of The Nord. As the others placed trembling hands on their weapons Carain realized he had forgotten to bring one of his own. He bit the side of his cheek in order to focus while helping the girl over the railing.

The ship looked like any standard transport ship. The only difference were the royal flags hanging from the masts, indicating that it carried nobility. To Black Dok it acted as a target, wheras other sailors would stay clear of it.

"Find lanterns mates," Dok quacked and pointed to various points of the ship. Buhlo and Wyle scurried about and quickly located and lit the lanterns.

Warm yellow glow cut through the inky blackness of the moonless night and Carain had an uneasy sensation come over him. He thought he could hear the muted sounds of a clapper gently rolling against the side of a bell.

"It is here," Dok said and tried to smile, but the action only twisted his face into a sinister grin. "We split up here," he continued. "Carain go with the whisperer and Bulho, Wyle and the twins with me."

Carain, Sona, Buhlo and the child remained above deck and were ordered to look for survivors, while Dok and his party searched for the bell. How the captain had figured he would get the object over to The Vereem he had not revealed, but Buhlo seemed convinced they would keep The Nord for the time being.

"Where are your parent's quarters," Sona asked the girl. "There might be clues to their whereabouts there."

"I find it unlikely," Carain replied as he slowly opened the ornate doors under the quarter deck. "Are you expecting to find a note from them explaining what happened?"

"No," Sona cast him an offended look. "There might be remnants there."

"The child said they were all gone when she woke up," Buhlo threw a thumb over his shoulder. "If people leave in such a hurried that they forget their young I doubt there are any clues."

The door opened up to a narrow hallway, barely wide enough for two creatures to walk side by side. There appeared to be several cabins, unusual for a vessel of this kind, but maybe a simple fix in order to house Lord and Lady Folg with space for the captain and the girl. The doors were all ajar, slowly moving to and fro, in time with the rhythm of the vessel. Carain, glanced over to the others and placed a finger to his lips. His eyes narrowed at the low creaking of wood, attempting to determine if it was merely the natural sounds of a ship, or if someone moved along the floorboards. He moved his hands to his belt but remembered he had neglected to bring a weapon. The girl pointed to a simple door at the end of the hallway and Carain nodded, motioned for Bulho to take the lead. The simian abandoned his lantern and replaced it with a boat ax.

With great force Bulho shouldered the door and leapt into the room. The others watched in silence as he looked from side to side, waiting for an ambush that did not come. When his shoulders slumped, and he relaxed his stance Carain joined him.

"Empty?" Sona asked.

"Very much so," Carain replied. "It would appear they left in a hurry. There is a meal prepared, though untouched."

"A bed unslept in," Buhlo added as he wandered the small, yet fancy quarters.

Sona, holding the hand of the child followed carefully, raising her staff to sense the room.

"I can feel great fear here," she said with her eyes closed. "It is so palpable that you should be able to perceive it as well Carain."

The first mate felt no need to reach out and touch the dread. He could sense something. It prickled the hairs on the back of his neck. Like an electrical charge from a lightning strike.

"I am not convinced this was a peaceful escape," Buhlo pointed his ax to a dark crimson stain that covered the otherwise white tablecloth and had dripped on the floor.

"I am inclined to agree," Carain walked over to over-turned vanity, jewelry and fancy clothes strewn about.

"Let us investigate the other cabins," Buhlo eyed the little girl, who averted her gaze.

Finding the hatch leading below deck proved quite easy. Most vessels were built the same. Black Dok lead his party of Wyle and the albino twins past the living quarters and down to the subdecks. Folks said he could smell riches. That the tiny holes in his bill had guided him right on more than one occasion, both Hampus and Ward had experienced it firsthand. Even though his captain oozed confidence and seemed afraid of nothing or anyone Hampus could not shake the uneasy feeling he felt in his gut. His mother had always claimed both her sons were magically inclined. Most set it down as being their lack of pigment, but Hampus knew he had sensitivities. They washed over him now, like alarm bells warning him of something.

The twins took the rear with their short swords at the ready. Every little creek or movement from a ships rat startled them and, in the darkness, their pink eyes darted from side to side in a nervous dance.

Dok halted in front of a simple door at the far end of the ship. They had wound around in a labyrinthine mass of crates and debris. Wilde assumed they were lost, not as confident in the rumors regarding her captain, but now they seemed to have found their goal.

"It is in here," Dok pressed his tiny body against the weathered wood. "I can feel it."

The four of them could hear it sing from the other side as the clapper rolled back and forth. It felt oddly soothing. The bare hint of a melody intermingled with the darkness around them and the bobbing of the ship.

"We enter," Dok said and slowly slid his sickle from his belt.

The bell lay only partially covered by a large piece of fabric. In the lantern light it looked like it might be a discarded sail. Unsecured by any ropes it rolled slightly, lazily like an obese lord lounging on his gilded couch. The glow from their lights reflected in the polished metal, giving them all a golden shine.

"By the great duck," Dok rubbed his hands together. Almost foaming at the mouth. "This is a treasure and no mistake."

"How do we get aboard The Vereem?" Wyle touched the metal with her paw. Careful to retract her claws.

Dok snapped his bill. "Good question Wyle. We might have to leave Carain here with a crew to sail back to Atrista."

He moved closer to the bell and grabbed the clapper.

"This is pure gold, mates. I am going to be rich."

He dropped it and the bell sounded a dull, deafening gong. The vibrations reverberated through them and soundwaves crashed against their chests, like real waves crashing against the shore. As it petered out and they regained their faculties another sound met them.

A high-pitched cry pierced the very fabric of the ship. Rattling the timbers and threatening to shred their ears.

"Where did that come from?" Ward got into a fighting stance.

"I am not sure if it came from outside or inside," Hampus replied.

Wyle raised her lantern and held it towards the entrance to the storage room. The flame flickered and went out. Just like the others. They were in total darkness.

"You heard that, right?" Carian poked his head out from the captain's cabin.

The others met him in the narrow hallway. They had all heard the sound of the bell and now the wail of some otherworldly beast.

"Does that sound like..." Sona turned to where the girl had been. She had vanished.

"Where did the child go?" Buhlo asked.

Then their lanterns expired.

Carain felt something brush against him in the darkness. He raised his fists in attempt to defend himself.

"Stay together," he cried through the commotion.

Something moved around them and there were flashes of blue light exploding here and there. He thought he could see the little girl appear at every flash. Then Buhlo screamed.

The hallway exploded with bright light as Sona raised her staff. Blood stained her white dress and her face had turned white. Buhlo lay slumped against the wall and next to him stood the girl.

She had transformed into something else. Her clothes torn as four claw- like limbs protruded from her stomach and held her aloft. Six dark eyes stared back at him and under what used to be her nose a terrible maw with rows of jagged teeth snapped. Blood stained her black lips, and Carain could see a hint of black fur caught between the teeth. The girl wailed and darted past them. He tried to catch her as she passed, but her movements were too fast. He turned to Sona.

"Are you injured?"

She touched her body. "No more than scratches I think," there were long tears in the fabric.

Carain came to kneel by the simian who no longer breathed. A large chunk of flesh where the thing must have bit Buhlo now missing from the neck.

"What was that?" Carain turned to the Whisperer.

"I have never seen such a thing in my life," Sona replied. "The bell seemed to have called to it.

"That is what happened to the crew and passengers," Carain rose, grabbing Buhlo's boat ax. "Not securing the bell caused it call the monster from the depths and it took the body of the girl."

"We need to stop it," Sona looked at Carain. "If it can shift then we cannot let it reach land."

"You can see in the dark Wyle," Dok told the catton. "Get us out of here."

Wyle hesitated, but knew it to be true. The dry had rattled them all and they felt the need to escape the ship, or at least reach the top deck. She slowly moved through the door, clutching a knife at her side.

"Let us just stay together," Ward said in a shaky voice.

"What are you afraid of?" Dok snorted.

"Whatever cried is not of this world," Ward continued. "I think it has something to do with the ship being abandoned.

"These are uncharted waters," Hampus added. "Who knows what vile things live below."

No sooner had those words been spoken and the party crossed the threshold into the maze of ship cargo, then they hurried the scurrying of something in the dark. It did not sound like the tiny claws of rats, no, rather more like metal points clicking against the hard floor.

Wyle tried scanned the area and though she could see a shape move from behind one crate to another. He whispered to the others to stand back but stay vigilant. Then, as soon as she took another step forward, she felt it. A great force barreled into her chest. It sent Wyle back and it knocked the wind out of her lungs as she struck the hull of the ship. A tiny, but hard body pinned her against the wall, the scent of salt water mixed rotten seaweed filled her nostrils. As soon as her breath return, she called for the others to run, while at she attempted to stab at the tiny frame trapping her. She realized it was the little girl pushing pinning her and could not understand how such a tiny thing possessed such strength. Then it raised its head. Six dark orbs looked up at her as two crab like appendages held her back. The creature opened a bloody mouth, howled in the dark then sunk its teeth into Wyle's chest.

Dok, Hampus and Ward fumbled in the darkness. Crashing into crates and objects. Desperately trying to find the exit. They heard the wail of something and then the guttural cry of Wyle as she died.

Without direction Ward suddenly fell over the stairs leading to the sleeping quarters. He scrambled, slipping, falling, hurting his knees on the wooden steps. They heard another screech and that hideous clattering approach them. Ward flung himself from the hatch, followed by Dok. The light from an emerging moon shone from the hatch leading to the deck and Black Dok waddled past as fast as he could, but Ward waited for Hampus. A white hand emerged from the dark and Ward grabbed it.

"Come brother," he called.

A shrill cry, the only answer he received. His brother's face came into view, the white light illuminating it, almost making Hampus seem transparent. Blood bubbled up from inside him and erupted like a geyser from his mouth. Ward through he could see the shape of the little girl they had rescued tearing through Hampus' back.

"Stand back," Dok cried as he flung a lit lantern

down the hatch.

Ward scooted back, tears in his eyes, knowing all too well that his brother's fate was sealed. Another cry as flames danced from below.

"There are containers of tar down there," Dok laughed. "This ship will be the fiery grave of that beast. We can recover the bell from the depths."

Carain and Sona emerged from under the quarter deck at the same time as Dok and Ward climbed out from the hatch, chased by fire.

"What is happening?" Carain cried to them over the creaking of the ship.

The flames had spread faster than Dok had imagined. The Nord rolled to the side and the bell rang out as moved with it. Several shrieks replied all around them.

"There are more of them," Sona said, her staff still aglow.

"Back to the Vereem," Dok ordered, before they take it as well.

The Ward's chest exploded in a shower of dark red. One single crab like claw protruding from him. The girl, charred remains of clothes falling from her as the other limbs carried her above them. Still transforming, her body contorting and writhing as red scales replaced the soft dark skin. It cried to the heavens as the bell continued to toll. Her kin answering all around them.

Carain imagined he could hear scraping against the hull as the fire crackled.

"We need to get out of here," he said.

"I am with you on that score," Dok winked and suddenly grabbed Sona's arm.

Before any of them could react, he dragged her around and sent her rolling towards the beast approaching them on the deck. Carain shouted and Sona howled when the creatures crushed the Whisperer's head with one evil sounding crunch.

"Are you mad?" Carain said and raised the boat ax at Dok.

"You will not slay me Carain," Dok smiled and walked past him. "You owe me your life."

Carain sighed. His shoulders slumped and he dropped the ax to his side. Dok motioned for a crewman at The Vereem to through him a rope. A group had gathered to watch the spectacle. The creature slipped the limp body of Ward from its claw and scuttled across the deck.

"I am going to need time to flee Carain," Dok looked at the first mate. "Be a dear and buy me some time."

Carain nodded. Hefted the ax in his hand and closed his eyes. The beast came at them and with a war cry drowned out by the bell sounding, he ran towards the thing.

The burning Nord lit up the night sky, coloring the water a bright orange. Smoke rose up towards the moon as the bell continued to toll with every movement of the vessel. The creatures deep below the slight waves replied in a continuous wail. It sounded almost melodic after a while.

Black Dok ran a feather finger over the point of his sickle and snapped his bill together. Now he would have to find another treasure and more crew. He sighed and headed to his quarters.

COLOSSUS

E.L. GILES

"Storm! Storm!"

The voice shouted relentlessly, hovering like a curse I could neither escape nor fight. The voice sounded far away, distorted and unearthly, disturbing my already fitful sleep. Every sway of the cabin and every gust of wind brought on the worst of the nightmares—sea monsters, giant tentacles hurtling against the side of the ship. I opened my eyes, startled after a particularly loud thump snatched me from my reveries. The door was slamming against the wall, and a cold, sizzling draft of air invaded the room. I had raised into a seated position, rubbing my face and was getting used to the dim light in the room, when I noticed the frame of a man in the doorway, standing still and staring at me. He said nothing. Behind him reigned the deepest darkness I had ever seen. It was as if the ship had sunken into an unfathomable abyss.

"Yes?" I said, regaining my wits after a particularly displeasing chill caused me to tremble uncontrollably. The man stayed silent, which troubled me greatly.

I detached the lantern I'd hung beside my cot and waved it before me, illuminating the features of the man. His eyes were black, like two bottomless pits, and his skin was so white it was nearly translucent. I didn't recognise him. With a face like that, I would have remembered him. A sudden commotion on the deck drew my attention, and for a moment, I watched over the man's shoulder at the crew running to and fro, panicked. When I watched the man again, he had disappeared, leaving in his wake a strange, baleful aura of mystery.

"Storm! A storm is coming!" The voice entered the cabin with ghastly echoes, clear and loud. Distressing. Dreadful.

I jumped out of my cot and was greeted by my second officer, Albert Fischer, who erupted into my cabin unceremoniously.

"I know," I said before he could speak. I ran outside onto the deck, where the crew was waiting for my orders.

I knew the great *Colossus* could fight the impending storm, for the vessel had been built to resist every tempest the world could know. Typhoons and cyclones, white squalls and thunderstorms alike. There was nothing the ship couldn't handle. And yet, as I stared out across the sea and all around me, terror began to overwhelm me.

"What are your orders?" asked Albert, elevating his voice to be heard over the thunderclaps and piping wind.

Everywhere, giant cumuli piled up in monstrous mountains of madness, their wombs hosting the chaos that awaited to slaughter us. On all sides, sheets of blinding rain descended, plummeting onto the surface of the sea like boulders falling down a cliff. The noise was deafening, maddening, driving some of the men to clasp their hands over their ears and fall to their knees, unable to bear the pain any longer.

We were surrounded by this impenetrable wall, beyond which lightning bolts flared through the sky, illuminating the world around us with cosmic hues of violet and red. I had no options. Stopping and waiting for the storm to pass was useless. We had tried to do so already, and this was the result; we were trapped inside this pandemonium. The crew was exhausted, angry, edgy, desperate. Going back whence we'd come was impossible. And fighting it would be sheer madness. I was beginning to think that a curse floated over the great *Colossus*.

"I don't know," I finally said. Albert's eyes darkened. That wasn't the answer he'd expected, not the one the entire crew waited for. Surely not the one I'd wanted to come up with. Over Albert's shoulder, a familiar face caught my attention—the stranger who'd visited my cabin. "Who's this?"

Albert frowned and spun around, following the path of my outstretched hand. He searched, not seeing what I intended to show him.

"Who?" he said. My shoulders dropped.

"The man right—" I searched, but the man had once

again disappeared. "What the hell?"

When a harsh tremor traversed the deck from stern to bow, causing it to break right where the man stood, it became clear to me. Whoever the man was, with his presence, had come an inexplicable blight. First, the tempest had seemed to activate with his presence, and now, strange tremors and tides as high as three-story buildings buffeted the ship, causing it to rock wildly from one side to the other. I gripped the railing for balance when I heard someone cry, "Man overboard!"

I twisted my neck and gazed over my shoulder. There he was again, his face piercing through the impenetrable wall of rain and dark shapes. No matter the great debacle happening all around me, I couldn't avoid seeing him and his grave, awful face. I was filled with an unspeakable terror as I waited for the next calamity to fall upon us.

"Hold on!" I yelled to the panicked crew. The stranger wasn't done with us. Increasing the fury of the elements, the stranger kept on challenging the indestructibility of the *Colossus*. A violet lightning bolt descended from the sky and stroke on the mainmast, breaking it in half and setting its sails ablaze. And I watched, powerless, as the mast crashed onto the deck, killing as many men as the claws of destruction could reach. Cries elevated all around me like a horde of banshees riding malignant tides, shrieking painfully and desperately.

The stranger's presence grew omnipresent, ominous, and suffocating. His hands waved over me like a puppeteer pulling the strings of our fate. In front of me he stood, advancing toward me relentlessly. Behind me was the gluttonous mouth of the sea. The man's pace was steady, certain, and heavy. His advance unstoppable. And I retreated until I found myself pressed against the handrails. I was now face-to-face with the stranger, searching for my reflection in his black eyes. He placed his skeletal hands against my chest, and with a power that took the air from my lungs, pushed me from the *Colossus* into the water.

The water assaulted my skin with millions of icy shards, dulling my senses. I looked up at the distorted shape of the ship, which was succumbing to the flames. But I felt nothing. Everything was calm here. Silent. Dark. And I didn't understand why it had all so abruptly ended.

I saw nothing, only felt my body being dragged out of the water and pulled onto solid ground. I coughed and gasped for air, wriggling and floundering around in an attempt to get rid of the pain assailing my entire body.

"Who… who are you?" I asked, opening my eyes. Here he was again, the stranger, with his pallid features. He wore a wide black hat that seemed to belong to another age. It flapped loosely over his eyes, casting a shadow that exaggerated the sharp lines of his cheekbones and the depth of his eye sockets, giving him the look of a *Dia de Los Muertos* festival goer. I was frozen with fear. "*You!* Where… where am I? What do you want?"

The man crouched, grinning. "New York," he exclaimed with an accent I didn't recognise.

"New York?" I raised into a sitting position. The rain plummeted on my head, cold and penetrating, but I felt nothing other than horror. Disarray, loss. Was I going insane? "New York…What did you do? Have we gone adrift?"

"Me? I did nothing," he said.

"How can we be here, then?"

"Easy. You never left New York, Thomas. Never!"

"What? No. You're wrong. We were in the middle of the Atlantic Ocean—three days away from anywhere. And you were there too." I pointed at the man, my hand trembling, my accusation uncertain.

The man burst out laughing. His voice echoed freely in the open air, deep and evil. I looked all around me, my gaze stumbling over the cranes and filthy barracks surrounding me. When I looked back to the man, baffled, he was gone—gone, along with the *Colossus*.

GALLOWS MAST

PETER J. FOOTE

The Harbinger sensed the life within her hull and found them acceptable. She called upon the evil which lived within its timbers and summoned forth the tainted fog; it was time to feed.

"Where did this blasted fog come from? And what is that smell?" First Lieutenant Rory called out from his position at the prize ship's wheel, as the sails hung as limp as their hopes to cash in on their war prize.

"Isaacs! Keep the Goose in sight and signal them requesting they come alongside." Rory shouted, and watched as the fog began swallowing their mother ship. "Isaacs, you fool, get their attention! We can't afford to lose them!" the Lieutenant cursed and ran across the deck, breaking the thin tendrils of fog which oozed from the timbers and lay like a cat seeking to trip its owner.

Coming up behind the crewman who was shouting and waving blue and red signal flags, Lieutenant Rory added his voice to the general din and even pulled free his pistol from its brace. The fog absorbed the hollow 'woof' of the discharged gun, and in minutes they lost the Warship Goose from sight.

"That's not natural, Lieutenant. How'd the Goose have full sails and we be dead in the water?" One of the prize crew called out.

First Lieutenant Rory jammed his smoking pistol into his brace and rested his hand upon its mate as he turned to his crew.

"Don't be flapping your lips, Higgins, your teeth will fall out." Rory said with forced humour in his voice, and the prize crew laughed, easing the mood. "It's true that the fog took unawares, but we're tougher than a bit of fog, aren't we?" A weak chorus of agreement sounded from the fourteen men. "The Goose will realise they lost us and heave to and they won't find us sitting on our thumbs."

The setting sun was a hazy orange orb that failed to burn through the thick fog. Collectively the prize crew of the Harbinger shivered and shuffled together like cattle, fearing the cry of the wolf.

"Quit that nonsense, men. You volunteered for this post, and we all know the King's shilling doesn't come easy. Light the lanterns, I want a man at bow, wheel and stern keeping a lookout for the Goose or a break in the fog. Ring the ship's bell every minute and listen for any reply. The rest of us will sample the stores of this vessel and break open a cask or two." Rory shouted. The forced bravo and promise of alcohol was enough to dislodge any doubts amongst the prize crew. None of the sailors noticed the slips of fog that wormed their way within the shadows and followed them below decks.

"Men. Stand and raise your cups." First Lieutenant Rory cried, and wooden benches scraped against stained boards as the prize crew stood. "We may never know what befell the crew of the Harbinger, and many aboard the Goose were too afraid to risk a similar fate, but you brave souls aren't!"

A chorus of shouts and cheers answered the first lieutenant as the prize crew drank from their cups and feasted upon the food and drink found within the abandoned Harbinger, they discovered the day before bobbing out at sea.

Before long, talk turned to the fate of the missing crew and how much the prize crew might receive for bringing a fully supplied and armed vessel to the King's flag. With the libations flowing, the crew failed to notice that the air temperature lowered, and the lanterns dimmed, the men just huddled closer and drank deep, putting their backs to the darkness.

The fingers of fog circled the boisterous men, snaking its way around legs that shivered and pulled away, and the Harbinger knew the time to feed would be soon.

Over the dim of his crew Lieutenant Rory paused in rising his glass of watered wine and listened, realising that the bell he had ordered rung had stopped sounding. "Those lazy brutes, I'll see to their lashing when we get back…" stumbling footsteps coming down the ladder from the main deck drew everyone's ear, and the men fell silent.

Higgins nearly fell as he came to a stop at the bottom of the steep stairs but stayed on his feet even if he swayed like a drunkard in the poor light.

"Higgins! Why aren't you at your post?" Rory shouted, and started forward, only to pause as the hairs on the back of his neck stood on end. "Higgins?" Rory repeated as his right hand slid to the pistol in his brace and his left grabbed the lantern from the table.

When the light struck Higgins, the assembly of men tumbled backward over their benches as they tried to flee.

First Lieutenant Rory forced himself to stand in place as he looked upon Higgins. Smokey tentacles of fog encircled each of the man's limbs like strings on a martinet, with the largest twisted around the man's neck like a noose. Rory stared into sightless eyes as the dead man danced with nothing but groaning timbers as his musical accompaniment.

In a twisted parody of a jig, the dead man danced as if boneless, his limbs flew out with wild abandon, and his protruding tongue flopped around like a dog on a hot day.

When his dance finally completed, the dead man gave a sloppy bow before the stunned assembly and the tentacles of fog ripped his limbs from his body as if tearing paper.

Covered in the blood and flesh from their former crew mate, the prize crew of the Harbinger screamed and struggled to get as far away from the quartered man as possible as the tentacles of fog waved the torn limbs around the galley in a twisted parody of life.

Gore splattered and shaking, Rory nevertheless drew his pistol, cocked the hammer and aimed at the thick tentacle which held the limbless man erect. Even as his bowels turned to water, and he felt reason flee his mind, his training held, and the musket ball struck true. It sliced through the fog with no effect and lodged itself in the wooden wall.

"Lieutenant! Snap out of it, man!" Isaacs shouted and grabbed the lieutenant as the tentacles of fog dropped the tattered pieces of the dead man and weaved their way into the gallery, searching for new playthings to feed upon.

Rory forced his eyes away from the disassembled Higgins, the man's torso and head leaned against the wall and stared at him as if judging him from beyond the grave. Willing his feet to move, Rory and Isaacs pushed and shoved the men who desperately tried to make their way forward, but not all were to make it.

Snaking its way through the milling men, the fog grabbed ankles and wrists, pulling bodies from the crowd. With every cry, comrades in arms would struggle to free the ensnared man, but they were no match for the supernatural strength of the Harbinger.

Of the eleven men who were in the gallery, only four made it to the forward hold. One by one it had dragged the others into the darkness, each man yelling for their mates to help them before their screams ended with flesh tearing and voices choked on gurgling blood.

"In, in, in!" Rory shouted, and grabbed the lantern that hung outside the forward hold before slamming the heavy door closed. His last view of the hall showed him a maze of writhing tentacles flowing towards them faster than a man could run. "Barricade that door and get the top hatch open, we'll make for the rowboat!" Rory shouted, waving the discharged pistol for emphasis. While two of the crew struggled to drag crates in front of the door, Rory hurried the lantern over to Isaacs, who struggled against the top hatch.

"It's no go Lieutenant, it's secured tight."

"Nonsense, we'll get a pry…" cries of pain cut off whatever else Rory had been about to say, as he turned to find the two men at the door struggling for their lives against tentacles of fog that wormed their way through the walls with more appearing by the second.

The padlocked top hatch thumped and shook for several more moments, as terrified voices shouted for aid, but soon the last traces of life left the Harbinger and the ship relished its most recent meal, having gorged itself like a lion after taking a wildebeest on the savanna.

Satisfied, the ship dispelled the tainted fog it had called forth and allowed the ocean currents to carry it to its next prey, content that in time it would feed again, but now it was time to rest.

"And why do we need to take down these poor buggers?" Damas said as he looked up at the bodies swinging from the ancient oak and clutched his filthy hands together.

Faces black with rotting blood, crow-pecked eyes wept down pock-marked cheeks and peered through the shroud that only the dead could pierce while listening to the exchange below.

"We need the ropes, fool!" Hoche said, his voice raspy from cheap booze and pipe smoke. "If you want to escape this piss-poor outpost before the English burn it to the ground, then we need those ropes!" With rough shoves and kicks, Hoche got his crew of fellow deserters of the French navy into action.

The setting sun provided sufficient light as Damas and Marien scurried up the oak. Thin canvas shoes and callused fingers found easy purchase. Years at sea made this simple work for them. They begin the distasteful task of untying the long lengths of hemp rope that served as nooses for the unfortunate souls who swung like spoiled fruit.

"You know," Hoche said to his fellow deserters. "I might have sailed with that bloke," pointing to the body that was missing the index and ring finger on its left hand. "I think that's Pitchfork Patty. He always had sticky fingers and lost one every time he got caught dipping into the grog. Looks like he lost more than a finger this time. I hope our luck is better."

Feeling a chill that was more than the early spring air, Hoche looked up at the large oak and shuddered. By far the grandest tree within the area, the tree dominated the landscape.

It almost feels like it's leaning over me and staring,

judging us. Like some preacher leaning down from his pulpit, Hoche thought and took several steps backward until he was no longer beneath the canopy of the oak.

Noticing that the others of his gang had seen his withdrawal, Hoche lashed out. "Fools, they can't hurt you now, their souls are standing judgment and unless you want to join them," Hoche drew forth a rusty officer's sword from his belt. "Get in there and get those ropes, we have no time to spare."

As the first of the hanged men struck the frozen spring ground, bloated body split open like overripe fruit, putrid juices splashed on clothes and clung to nostrils. Young Janvier collapsed to his knees and threw up. Shaking his head, Hoche grabbed Osmin, and they began the ugly task of removing the noose from the poor soul. They didn't pause as another body plummeted to the ground, bursting like a melon, and the sound of retching filled their ears.

Worn-out shoes splashed through slush. The feet of the five deserters crushed the delicate ice crystals around the edges of puddles as they left behind the woodlands and reached the beach.

Weighted down by the long coils of rope, each man took a deep breath of clean sea air to purge the stink of death and decay hanging off them. The act of salvaging the nooses played on each. How Hoche had to apply his old sword to separate heads from bodies to free the ropes. Young Janvier fainted, and even thrice-damned Damas mumbled a hasty prayer over the remains they left rotting under the oak.

But all that was behind them now. Starlight reflected off the waves of the harbour as the high tide lapped against the rock shore.

As the deserters threw down their death stained burdens, Hoche hissed at them and pointed to the glowing light from the besieged town in the distance.

"Quiet, you fools. Remember how sound carries on the water. Have you lost all your sea-knowledge after a couple weeks ashore?"

Voices mumbled and cursed, and Hoche ignored it. "Janvier, if you're done puking your guts, come help me." Seeing the inexperienced man hesitate, Hoche placed his hand on his sword hilt and even in the starlight. The message was unmistakable. Janvier rushed to obey.

Away from the others and their tainted burden, Hoche dragged pieces of driftwood and cut boughs away from a hump in the bank to expose a small dinghy.

"Quit standing there like an officer and come do some work." Hoche hissed, and Janvier rushed over. Even in the dark, his eyes are full of fear.

"Lad, why did you desert? The rest of us were for the noose or axe ourselves and living on borrowed time, but Damas said you only had a lashing coming your way."

Dragging the camouflage off and helping to turn the dinghy over, Janvier spook. A voice with precious little time spent in the realm of adulthood said, "I was trying to do right by her. She said the babe was mine and if I could get the coins, we'd be together..." Janvier trailed off as Hoche chuckled.

"Lad, you won't be the last man who ran away in shame after a woman's made a fool of him, but it might be the last for you."

Shaking his head and dismissing the young man from his thoughts, Hoche clucked his tongue. The flat sound carried, and in moments the rest of the deserters with their burdens scrambled along the shoreline.

"You can't be serious, Hoche." Damas said as his weather-beaten hands grasped the oarlock. "No way we survive open water in this. I can smell the worm rot in the hull. What you playing at?"

Instead of reaching for his sword, Hoche moved in and leaned against the dinghy, its hull ground against the beach rocks.

"Lads, you know me. We've sailed together, whored together, and drunk together. Trust me in this and we'll all do it again." As the deserters mumbled amongst themselves, Hoche continued. "Sure, you could flee inland and avoid the British troops out there, but we're sailor's lads. We won't survive the wilds. We could slip back into town and shelter behind log barricades and wait to be burned out or starve to death. Or we could risk open water. Slip past our old shipmates under the flag of France and make a dash for warmer weather in the south before the English fleet traps us here. What say you?"

Knowing they had no alternative; the men cursed and swore under their breath but grasped the gunnels and carried the dinghy to the water and heaped the stolen cordage inside.

Shivering and soaked, the five men pushed off

and with the lapping waves to cover the splashing of the oars, they rowed out into the harbour.

"God take you, Hoche!" Damas snarled and reached for the leader of the deserters. The dinghy rocked; water poured over the gunnels of the battered craft.

Twisted fingers broken from a life of rough labour and misadventure gripped Hoche's stained wool collar. "By the Holy Mother, what are you thinking bringing us to the Harbinger? That ship is cursed, don't you know?" cried Damas, his voice echoed down the harbour.

"Shut up fool," hissed Hoche, "do you want to signal the township to what we're doing?"

Hoche pried the fingers away from his throat as the others pulled Damas away and waited until rocking dinghy resumed its steady bob of the waves in the harbour before speaking.

His voice just above a murmur, Hoche spoke. "What did you think we would do? Think! We need a ship to gain our freedom and the Harbinger is the only one not being used to keep the English out of the harbour."

The twinkling stars showed the look of murder on Damas's face, but he kept his voice low. "So, your grand idea is to sail a cursed and run aground schooner through the blockage with five men? I'd rather take my chances inland."

All rowing stopped as the other deserters listened to the decision that would seal their fate.

Opening his arms as if drawing in all the men and not just Damas, Hoche explained his choice.

"Lads, it's true something foul happened on the Harbinger, I was one of the poor sods pressed into stripping her of everything useful. Where do you think this dinghy came from? Passengers and crew were missing and no sign of what happened. But she's our only hope of living as free men."

"She's still run aground on that sandbar Hoche, how do ya mean us to free her if the French navy couldn't." snapped Damas.

"Lads, don't forget my life is on the line as well here, and I mean to die in me bed with a woman and full bottle of rum." Hearing a couple chuckles, Hoche felt the men were turning to his side.

"They pressed all the petty officers into stripping the Harbinger. We took her cannons, shot, rope, sail, and even a good portion of her ballast to raise her, to no avail. But god is with us tonight, lads." Hoche said and pointed to the moonless sky above them.

"New moon, full moon, high water at noon." Janvier muttered, the growing smile on his face clear even in the moonless sky.

Nodding, Hoche echoed the smile. "That's right lads, I stashed a couple sails and provisions while we were stripping the ship, but wasn't able to grab any line, that's why we need that." He said, pointing at the long pieces of gallows ropes piled around their feet.

"With the tide high, skilled hands, and a bit of luck, we should be able to sail the Harbinger out of the harbour and through the navies lines." Holding up a hand to forestall the coming argument, he continued. "Yes, it's possible we could take fire from our former mates, but we'll be running without lamps, coming from behind, and they won't give chase since they know the English are due any day now."

Pausing, Hoche met the eyes of his fellow deserters, their faces shadowed, shoulders slouched.

"Lads, what say you?"

Damas grunted and said, "To oars, lads and let's hope fortune favours the bold."

The deserters resumed rowing. The black outline of the Harbinger grew closer, starlight illuminated the narrow band of fog where ship met water.

"You can feel the evil that lives in this ship. And why does it stink like a flooded graveyard?" Janvier whispered as the young man wiped his palms on his grubby trousers.

"Quit moaning and get to work hauling up the rope, fool." Hoche scolded.

Leaning into the Harbinger's list, Hoche watched as his skeleton crew of deserters struggled to hoist the stolen and salvaged ropes, they could get their hands on, including the collection that did former duty as nooses.

What a miserable group of sailors to work with, but such is life. Hoche thought and shook his head.

"What do we do with the dinghy, tow it behind?" Damas asked as they tossed the last of the rope into a pile.

"We can't afford to waste the line, plus as you said,

it's rotted with worm and won't float much longer. Let 'er drift." Hoche said and waved Damas over to him. Walking to the ship's wheel, Hoche gripped the fellow deserter's shoulder in a tight grip, looked to make sure that the others aren't listening, leaned in and whispered.

"Can I trust you, Damas? We can do this, but it won't be easy."

Shadowed eyes stare for a long time until Damas grunted and nodded.

"Good. Now come with me and we'll get what I squirreled away when the others were busy trying to free the ship."

Calling over his companion's shoulder, Hoche pitched his voice low. "You lads splice that rope into usable lengths. The starlight should be enough for ya. Damas and I are going for the sails and check for hull damage. And by the Holy Mother, be quiet!"

Satisfied that they heard his orders, Hoche and Damas made their way to the forward hold of the schooner. Narrow and dark walkways made the men stumble but having spent most of their miserable lives aboard ships, they got to forward hold with no problem.

"What is that evil smell? Did the ship have livestock onboard?" Damas mumbled, his hand over his face.

Ignoring him, Hoche bent down, scrambled in the dark until they heard the faint 'ting' of glass. "There you are!" he muttered and grunted over a flint and steel until an oil lamp caught light. Fingers of tainted fog reached out of the darkness and caressed the legs of the two deserters.

"God, it's as cold as ice down here, I can't stop shivering." Damas said and rubbed his arms.

The flickering lamplight shone off the freshly hammered nails securing the narrow hatch to the forward hold.

"Hoche, I be thinking you haven't been telling us everything." Damas whispered as Hoche thrusted the lamp into his shaking hands.

Ignoring his fellow deserter, Hoche drew his rusty sword and stabbed it into the gap between hatch and frame. Over the groaning of tortured timber, he cast a glance at the pale faced Damas and sighed.

"If the Harbinger be cursed or not, I truly don't know. I was part of the party that boarded her after she drifted into the harbour and run up on the sandbar." Screeching raised in pitch as the leverage of the sword pried the nails free and the hatch flew open. The smell of rotting blood caused each man to gag. Tendrils of fog raced into the forward hold, unseen in the flickering light.

Spitting onto the plank floor, Hoche thrusted his now bent sword back through his belt and continued. "All I know is that when this hold was first opened, the found the remains of fourteen bodies, each torn apart as if drawn and quartered, the limbs in one pile, heads and torso in another. It looked like they had tried to barricade themselves inside, but whatever had torn them to shreds found a way in. The officers ordered us to never breathe a word of what we saw, not that a soul would want to describe it. After we carted the bodies to shore, they tasked me with sealing the hold, but before I did,

I stashed what I could in here. I could tell which way the wind was blowing, the English were on their way, and our forces caught with their britches down. I figured having a backup plan won't hurt."

Taking the lamp from Damas, Hoche bent down and entered the stinking hold.

Damas made the sign of the cross on his breast and followed, his breath fogging in the cold air.

"Have you fools got those lines spliced yet? The tides nearly full, we won't get a second chance." Hoche said as he and a pale faced Damas struggled across the tilted deck of the Harbinger, loaded under the weight of canvas sails, the hooded lamp swung in Hoche's hand. Faint tendrils of fog snaked after them from below.

"Yeah Hoche, it's spooky. The line they strung those poor buggers up with spliced easy, almost as if they wanted to reconnect. You don't suppose..."

Hoche interrupted. "Fine, save the tale for later. Right now, I want you lads to rig us a couple jib sails at the bow, it won't be pretty but it's the best we can do with we have." The Harbinger bobbed on the sandbar as the waves of the high tide struck her hull. "Hurry lads. Forget being quiet, now we need speed."

As the five deserters hurried around the Harbinger in a frenzied race to hoist their make-shift sails, they didn't notice that the cursed Harbinger was awake and ready to feed once again. Pockets of icy air caused the deserters' breath to fog, and some shifting shadows were blacker than others, but the men failed to notice.

Lights on shore multiplied and voices echoed across the water as those within the besieged town noticed the actions on board the Harbinger. Voices and bobbing lanterns came together like drunken fireflies at the end of the wharf, and in moments they launched a skiff. Strong arms at the oars and a booming voice demanded more speed and the skiff to get closer, but not quick enough. The Harbinger was ready to sail.

"Good job lads, the Holy Mother is with us tonight. We need to monitor those sails. Trim them as best you can, I'll take the wheel." Hoche shouted and raced to the Harbinger's wheel. Slipping the noose from the handle, Hoche strained to turn the rudder of the trapped schooner as the faint breeze of the turning tide ruffled the Harbinger's jib sails. The ship leaned to her port side as the wind filled the make-shift sails. With his feet braced on the worn deck, Hoche steered. Like a bobbing cork, the Harbinger slid off the sandbar and was free to sail once again.

The five deserters cheered, but a volley of musket fire from the approaching skiff cut their celebrations short as the deserters ducked for cover. Soon the Harbinger outpaced the skiff and with it any concerns from behind them. Now it's the ones to the front.

"Hoche, what's your plan for getting by the blockade? We might outrun a skiff with men at the oars, but not our mates onboard warships." Damas said as the dark outline of the harbour mouth approached.

Leaning into the wheel, Hoche took a long time to respond.

"We sail straight through and make for open water,

trusting in luck and that the Holy Mother is watching over us."

Shaking his head, Damas responded. "But what's stopping our former mates from firing at us?"

Grunting with the effort of steering the limping ship, Hoche replied, "Nothing at all. To work you dogs, trim those sails and pray for your souls."

It would seem that the Harbinger was happy to be free again. Unbalanced and using makeshift rigging, the ship and the five deserters used the receding tide and burst out of the harbour at speed, straight into their former shipmates.

Voices and the clamour of bells from the three French ships defending the harbour mouth rung in Hoche's ears but putting as much distance between themselves and the warships consumed his attention.

"Damas! Are any of them giving chase?" Hoche yelled. "DAMAS!"

"One ship is pulling anchor, Hoche, I make it The Aurora."

"Curses! Trim those sails, lads. We need all the lead we can get." Hoche yelled and watched as his skeleton crew struggled to catch every breath of wind using make-shift sails and rigging.

The deserters were too busy to notice the rolling waves of fog that poured out of the Harbinger's portholes and hatches, though the men shivered as the bands brushed past them and flowed into the ocean.

"Cap'n?" Janvier said, his voice quivering. "Fog

is forming in the water and cresting the bow of the ship, there's a weird shine within it."

Fog? Any fog should be heading out to sea, not coming in with the tide. Hoche thought and risked a glance from the sails.

Sure enough, a wall of fog was forming around the bow of the Harbinger and spilled over the rails. With no other course of action available to them, Hoche crossed himself and allowed it to swallow the ship.

Thick fog encased the Harbinger and the men aboard her, wrapping them tight in its embrace, muffling all sound and filling their nostrils with its taint. Sails hung limp as the wind dropped off, and even the receding tide lost its strength. The abruptness of the transition startled the deserters as cries rung out from different locations. They lost the meagre starlight that was their guide, and the dark drew close.

"Shut up!" Hoche yelled. "Damas, grab the lantern and bring the men to the stern."

Raised voices and groaning timbers filled the fog-filled night until Damas and the other four deserters breached the darkness with the aid of the lantern and joined Hoche at the rudder. The flickering light of the lantern struggled to push back the oppressive gloom of the fog, forcing the five deserters to crowd together until their shoulders touched.

Grateful for the warmth of human bodies, Hoche blew into his freezing hands and met stare of the others.

"Lads, I won't lie to ya, this mysterious fog has me worried. Our only saving grace is that it's unlikely our former bunkmates will risk chasing us, but to be on the safe side, keep your voices down."

"What is that stink? It's like someone opened a grave." Janvier said through chattering teeth, the youth's eyes wide with fright.

Hoche and Damas exchanged a quick glance, each realising the smell was the same as that of the forward hold.

"It's probably something the tide stirred up, ignore it." Hoche hissed, "Now what we need to do is keep quiet and alert. Dawn isn't that many hours away and will burn off this fog, but until then we need to keep our eyes peeled. Janvier take the bow, Marien port side, Osmin the Starboard, and Damas the stern. Give a low whistle if you see a break in the fog or hear anything. Understood?"

Faces cast in flickering shadows looked to each other until Damas nodded, and as one, the deserters disappeared into the fog.

Keeping the lantern at his feet, Hoche kept one hand on the wheel, ready for any resistance from the water below, the other on the hilt of his sword.

"What was that?" Hoche called forward as a muffled cry floated its way to him.

"Osmin, Janvier, Marien, call out." Hoche ordered, and faint voices came from port and starboard.

"Damn Janvier, probably saw a spider." Hoche cursed and called Damas up from the stern. When his fellow deserter arrived, arms crossed and shivering, Hoche said. "Take the wheel. I need to check on Janvier, if he's lucky I won't toss him overboard."

Snatching up the lantern, Hoche saw that it's almost out of oil. He hoped there was enough until dawn, cursed, and made his way forward. The light from the lantern gave the fog a sickly yellow colour, which fitted with its terrible smell. Mindful of open hatches, Hoche nodded to Osmin as he materialised out of the fog, gripped the man's shoulder, and continued up the starboard side.

Following the curve of the Harbinger's railing, Hoche made it to the bow, only to find no Janvier. "Dammit lad, don't tell me you fell in." Hoche said, only to find his words swallowed by the fog. In slow sweeping arcs with his failing lantern, Hoche moved to the stern, looking for the lost deserter.

Cursing under his breath at the stupidity of youth, Hoche stumbled and jolted alert. Lifting their makeshift sail from the deck, Hoche cursed.

"Lads to me, the damn gallows ropes let go and we lost the..." His words trailed off as a pocket of fog dissolved in front of him, leaving a dangling Janvier swaying from a noose. The youth's fingers clutched tight at the rope around his neck.

"By the Holy Mother!" Hoche shouted and crossed himself. "Lads! To me lads." Muffled shouts and a cut off cry were his only response. Shivering from more than the cold, Hoche raced towards the wheel and away from the dead man only to fall as he ran into the twitching legs of Marien, and can only stand there paralysed with shock as the man's last feeble struggles ceased.

Drawing forth his rusty sword, Hoche probed the

fog with its tip as he hurried to the wheel.

"Damas, you there?" Hoche called as the outline of the wheel materialised out of fog.

"Yay, what is all the noise? It sounds..." Damas's question turned into a gurgled cry and Hoche raced forward, sword held high.

Hoche's brain struggled to process what it saw. The dying lantern showed thick tendrils of yellow fog wrapped around Damas like a massive snake. Coil after coil of fog encircled the man, squeezing him tight, forcing the air from his lungs, his eyes wide and pleading. Hoche placed the lantern upon the deck and rushed forward and slashed the coils of fog surrounding his fellow deserter to no effect.

As he watched Damas struggle, something new emerged from the fog. A coil of rope with a noose on the end snaked its way along the worn decking. It slithered its way atop the coils of yellow fog and dropped itself over Damas's head.

The fog retracted from Damas. Hoche stepped forward to help, only to freeze mid-step as Damas gave a strangled cry as the rope jerked the deserter into the mist, his feet drumming the deck as he disappeared.

Hoche turned to give pursuit, only to face the fingers of yellow fog blocking his way.

"Come at me then fell beasts!" Hoche roared as he slashed like a whirlwind, his flickering shadow a twisted silhouette against the fog. Panting with exhaustion, Hoche continued swinging his sword, but every coil he slashed healed in an instant, and unlike him, it showed no sign of tiring. Just as he considered jumping overboard and risk drowning, Hoche saw his lantern sputter and die.

Without even the stars to guide him, Hoche dropped his sword and roared in anger.

"Captain! That odd fog bank is dissolving. There's a ship emerging, no sign of crew or sail. Ghost ship Captain."

"Don't be foolish, Rogers. General Quarters, General Quarters. All hands, man your battle stations!" The captain of the British warship yelled, but all for naught.

"My apologies, Lieutenant Rogers. There appears to be some truth to your statement." The captain said as the British warship came alongside the Harbinger and saw five men hanging from her masts. "It's a French trick to scare us. Take a detachment of marines over and secure the ship and make ready to have her towed. We can use her in the coming battle."

"And the bodies Captain?"

"Consign them to the waves to receive their final rest, it's the least we can do."

The Harbinger was content that more souls would soon walk her cursed decks. She followed behind, bobbing and waiting to feed again.

HAIR OF FLAME

G. ALLEN WILBANKS

"Captain, I regret having to inform ye. A stowaway has found herself a way onto the Spector."

Captain Arthur Jamison looked up from the logbook on the table in front of him. His pen paused mid-sentence, rising from the paper as his attention moved from his daily journaling to the young girl accompanying his first mate.

"Stowaway?" he asked. "Are you sure she didn't just wander away from her family?"

The first mate, Isaac Cullen, glowered; his heavy black eyebrows drawing together to almost touch at the bridge of his bulbous nose. Arthur did not let the expression worry him overmuch. Glowering was Isaac's default expression. In fact, Arthur was unsure if he had ever seen the sullen old Scot smile in the four years he had known him.

"Aye. I'm sure. I found her hiding in the lower deck with the livestock. Her name doesn't match any we have on the manifest, and as to her parents… Well, perhaps ye'd best hear it from the lass' own lips."

Arthur nodded. He laid his pen on the table, picked up the log and blew a few gentle breaths on the pages to dry the new lines of ink. Closing the book, he set it beside the pen, then turned to give his full attention to the girl standing beside Isaac.

She was young, a child of nine or ten at first glance, or perhaps she might have been a few years older and merely small in stature to her age. Poor nourishment or disease could stall a child's growth, although she seemed healthy enough at present. Her limbs were long and thin, like the gangly legs of a pup waiting for its body to catch up with a recent spurt of growth. Smooth and pale, her delicate features were unblemished but for a dusting of fine freckles across her cheeks and over her nose. She was lovely as a youth, and her blue eyes and slightly pointed chin hinted she might one day be a remarkable beauty as an adult. The clothing she wore appeared unremarkable. Poor manufacture and cheap material, Arthur observed. Her dress was barely a brown sack hanging to her knees, with a hole to poke her head through and two poorly affixed sleeves covering her arms.

Neither her clothing nor her appearance was what grabbed Arthur's attention on first viewing, however. The most remarkable thing about her, the feature that caught the captain's eye immediately, was her hair. Long, wavy, and the colour of glowing embers, the girl's fiery tresses framed her face like a blazing halo.

"First thing to accomplish is an introduction, I suppose. I am Captain Arthur Jamison. You have met my First Mate, Mr Cullen. Might I have the pleasure of knowing your name, my little stowaway?"

"Rose," said the girl, grasping the hem of her rough dress to give a small curtsy. "I am Rose Long, sir. I apologise for coming aboard your ship without proper payment, but I did not know what else I might do to find my way to New York."

"Why do you need to be in New York? Does your family know where you are?"

The girl wiped a hand quickly across one cheek, trying to hide the single tear that had formed. "My family is why I am journeying so far. My parents secured passage for all of us to make the voyage to America, but we became separated. They went on without me, and now I must find portage on my own though I have no money or means to arrange proper travel."

"I see. How were you separated from your parents? I would think they might notice a child of theirs was of a sudden missing from their entourage."

A strange look crossed Rose's face. Her mouth twisted thoughtfully as she considered the captain's question. "I... I am not certain. We were together. We had booked passage and we… I do not know, sir. 'Tis quite strange. I found myself alone and remembered only that I must get to New York."

"Do you recall upon which ship they travelled?

Perhaps that will give me some idea of how far ahead of us they may be."

"Yes, sir. We hired the services of… The ship was… That is quite odd as well, sir, but I cannot remember the name of the ship. I am certain I once knew it."

"We ha' no room for her, Captain," interrupted the first mate. "We have supplies for our crew and the few passengers that belong with us. As a stowaway, the girl should be tossed o'er the side. And given the nature of the lass, sooner 'tis better."

Arthur understood his mate's concerns. The S.S. Spector was designed to carry cargo primarily. The few passengers they had aboard already shared cramped quarters and rationed food in order to make the fortnight-long voyage. One more mouth to feed could make a significant impact on resources if the trip were delayed for any reason. Still, the girl was only trying to reach her family, and he did not have the heart to see her die for the effort.

"No, Isaac. I think not. Rose has been our guest for four days already and we are none the worse for her presence. We are too far out to turn back to Portsmouth, and I will not be responsible for casting her off the ship. For as long as Miss Long is aboard my ship, she will be my guest and I will see her safely to New York."

"But, sir!" Isaac paused, glancing uncomfortably at the girl beside him. Stepping closer to the captain and lowering his voice, he continued. "Do ye not see the colour of the lass' hair? Like the flames of hell about her head. The girl is a curse to any vessel she sets foot upon and would like to be the death of us all. Ye cannot keep her aboard."

"She stays," Arthur stated firmly. "When we arrive in New York, I will place her with the proper authorities. They can reunite her with her family, send her home at their own expense, or keep her and put her to work in a brothel for all I care. But while she is my responsibility, I will not see her harmed or mistreated. For the next week or so, the Spector is as much her home as it is ours. Am I making myself understood?"

Isaac continued to look unhappy, but snapped a quick salute. "Aye, sir. And, where should I place your red-headed guest while she accompanies us?"

"There are no quarters unclaimed and I do not wish to have her wandering where she might get underfoot or disquiet any of the crew that could find her hair discomfiting." Arthur eyed Isaac meaningfully. "She has stayed this long with the livestock. I do not think another week in their presence will do her harm. Please make sure she is properly fed, however. I imagine she has been stealing grain from the animals thus far, and their rations are just as precious as our own.

"Does this meet with your approval, Rose," he asked the girl.

Rose nodded, then began to shiver. She wrapped her thin arms around herself in an effort to still her sudden distress. "Forgive me, sir. I am quite cold. It aches to the marrow of my bones and I struggle to find enough warmth to relieve it."

"Isaac, please see that our guest receives a coat and a blanket. The nights can be desperately cruel, especially for one so poorly attired."

"I'll take care of it. Blanket, food, and keep her out of sight, aye?"

"Yes. Thank you, Isaac."

Arthur watched the first mate escort the girl from his cabin. He turned back to his log, leafing through the pages to find his place, and recovered his pen. With this new discovery, there was more to add to today's journal than he had originally supposed.

Two uneventful days passed since Rose's discovery aboard the S. S. Spector. Arthur had all but forgotten about the girl since that initial encounter, knowing his first mate had seen to her care and that she was safely away from the crew and passengers somewhere in the lower holds of the ship. There were other, more immediate matters that demanded his time and attention. So long as the girl did not create a nuisance of herself, he found no cause to give her a second thought.

Rose, however, did not see fit to remain in hiding.

While attempting to settle a contentious dispute between two passengers over the disappearance of a small traveller's chest and its contents, Arthur found himself interrupted by one of the younger crewmen, gasping and panting from his haste to locate the captain. The runner informed him that Rose had appeared in the boiler room of the ship an hour or so earlier and was causing a disturbance among the men. Many of the crewmen refused to continue working in her presence, and two had gone so far as to accuse her of witchcraft, claiming she had materialised right in front of them from out of the air. They threatened to take matters into their own hands and toss her into the cold waters of the Atlantic if the captain did not deal with her directly.

Arthur excused himself from the argument with the promise that he would return to deal with the passengers' concerns at a later time, then followed the messenger back to the boiler room. His mood had already blackened and fouled that morning by the theft—only the most recent in a series—and it was not at all improved by the sight of the red-haired girl standing beside the massive boiler with her arms spread wide at her sides. Despite her promise to remain unseen, here she was, boldly flaunting her wild red hair in front of his crew. She had no shame, and clearly no understanding of the potential repercussions of her actions. The girl stood motionless, dismissive of the activity around her, her eyes squeezed shut and a beatific smile spread across her face.

"Rose!" he snapped. "You were told to stay out of the way. How can I protect you if you do not do as you are told?"

The child's eyes opened. Her smile did not waver. "I have been so cold. I can find no relief under blankets or clothing. The chill continues to burrow and gnaw in me despite all I do to relieve it. This place is gloriously warm. How could I stay away when it is the only comfort I have found in… oh, desperate ages? It touches me to my heart and lets me forget for a moment the ice that lives inside me."

Arthur knelt beside her, grasping her arms in his hands and shaking her to get her attention and to show the seriousness of his words. "There are those on this ship that would do you harm if they knew of your presence. You must stay as hidden as possible until I have you to New York. Can you not understand that?"

"I understand," she said. The smile finally faltering. "I know there are those that wish me ill because they believe me an omen of cursed luck. My intent was not to stir their ire. I wish only to be left alone and to reunite with my family."

"I am trying to do that for you, but you must do as you are told for me to accomplish this task. It assists neither of our goals if you insist upon bringing unnecessary attention to your presence on this ship."

Rose nodded solemnly. "Thank you for your help, sir."

Arthur released his grip on her arms and patted her shoulders more gently. "I do not mean to frighten you."

"There is cause to be frightened," Rose muttered ominously. "For I remember now how I came to be separated from my parents. I was pulled away. Two men dragged me from the arms of my mother. Men who feared my red hair on their ship."

"Your parents let the men take you?" Anger and disbelief coloured Arthur's expression.

Rose shook her head in a fierce negative. She wiped at the growing wetness in her eyes and stared at her feet as she recalled the event. "My mother fought, but the men threatened to harm her and my father as well if they did not allow me to be taken from them."

"What did the men do to you, Rose?"

"They… I was moved. They took me somewhere.

It was cold there, too. I don't remember where. My parents left without me."

"They boarded the ship and just left you?" Arthur asked, shocked at the idea they would leave their child behind to the mercies of two unknown men.

Rose nodded, her brows drawing together in confusion. "I do not think they had a choice. I can not recall why they left me, but I remember looking up to see my father and mother where they stood on the deck of the ship as it left. The Ca… The Call… No, I still do not remember the name of the boat. I saw the word painted along the side of the ship as it left me; tall white letters. My mother watched me, and I her; until we were lost to each other in the distance. I know they were sad, but they could not come back to get me."

"Why? Why couldn't they come back for you?"

"It was too late," Rose said sadly. Tears now flowed freely down her cheeks. "They had to keep going." She turned to face the boiler again, moving a step closer to the hot metal and the shimmering heat waves emanating from it. "So cold," she whispered.

Arthur pulled the girl into his embrace and held her tight for a moment. Just as quickly, he released her. "I can get you another blanket for your bedroll but, I'm sorry, you can't stay here. Will you go back to the lower deck?"

Rose nodded. "You are trying to be kind. Thank you. I am sorry I am causing you and your crew so much trouble. It will be over soon, however."

"Yes," he agreed. "We will be in New York in about a week and you will be back with your parents."

"We will all be together again," she said. Rose's smile returned, but the joy in her lips never touched the pale blue of her eyes.

Another two days passed. It appeared the crisis was past and the men who had witnessed Rose's visit to the boiler room returned to work with no further complaint. Arthur had once again put the girl's existence to the back of his mind and focused on the more immediate concerns of running a ship. The thefts had continued—mostly clothing and a few small valuables—and the passengers were growing more hostile, as they suspected the crew might have something to do with the disappearances of their property.

Arthur had begun interrogating the crewmen one at a time, attempting to discover his as yet unidentified thief, but he had found no likely suspects. Or rather, he had found too many.

It was during a rare quiet moment for Arthur, when Rose made her next appearance. Much as the first time he met her, Rose was dragged into his presence against her will.

The captain stood at the front of the foredeck, staring out over a pleasantly calm sea and silently praying the favourable weather would hold for another week. He was already calculating the time it would take to unload his current cargo, stock up for the return trip to Portsmouth, and set out. The stormy season was fast approaching, and Arthur wanted to be safely home with his wife and family when it arrived.

An agitated voice on the deck behind him disturbed his reverie. He turned to find two crewmen approaching him. One of the men held Rose tightly by one bicep, dragging her forcefully along at his heels. Arthur noticed Isaac following the men a few steps further back. The first mate's countenance looked more dour than usual; a bad sign.

"Captain, I have dark news and ill omens to report," said the man holding Rose's arm.

Arthur only vaguely recognised the man. He was a newer crew member, having worked on the Spector for only a few months. Oliver, he remembered, was the man's first name. He could not recall his surname.

"Please release your hold on the girl," Arthur said, mildly.

"Sir. She may run again, and I don't want her spreading her curse throughout the rest of the ship."

"Do I need to explain who is in charge of this vessel? I told you to release her."

When the man let go of Rose, the girl quickly side-stepped away from him but made no further attempts at escape. She wore only the sack dress today, Arthur noted. He wondered briefly what had become of the coat she had been gifted when they first discovered her.

"Now, what is this about a curse? Surely, you aren't afraid of a child simply because her hair is red."

"Captain," interrupted the first mate, stepping between the captain and the two crewmen. "Oliver was in the hold, feeding the livestock this morning when he discovered a score of goats and half again as many sheep dead of an unknown condition. They were all alive the night before, but at some time during the night, they expired. Suddenly, and without clear explanation. As he investigated, he found the girl asleep in a corner of the hold. What is equally disturbing is that he found her burrowed under a pile of clothing, gowns, and blankets that had previously been reported to us as stolen from those legitimately aboard the Spector. A search of her appropriated bedclothes further discovered items of jewellery and valuables passengers have advised us were removed from their rightful possession.

"Oliver properly retrieved all the missing property and brought the child immediately to me."

Isaac moved closer to the captain and lowered his voice. "I warned you, sir, that the girl would bring ill luck on us. She is cursed, and she is a thief. And now that curse has cost us much of our cargo, as well as the trust and good will of our passengers. I beg you to deal with this matter before she can spread her black touch further. The crew are already uneasy as rumours of the witch child spread among them, and it would not take much to turn them against us."

"You are doing it again!" Rose shouted at the two crewmen flanking her. "Just as before! I have not harmed any of your animals. I took clothing, I admit. I was so cold and wished to be warm, but I have taken ought else. You are blaming me for anything that goes wrong on your ship. Just like on the Callaway. They took me from my parents and sent me away because they were afraid. I will not let you send me away as well!"

"The Callaway?" asked Arthur, his attention fixated firmly on Rose. "That was the name of the ship your parents journeyed upon? I think you must be mistaken, child. It could not be the Callaway."

"Callaway," Rose repeated, insistently. "I saw the words on the side of the ship as it left me behind. I was so cold, barely able to keep my eyes open, but I saw the name as clear as I mark your faces before me now."

"The Callaway disappeared thirty years ago, Rose," Arthur told the angry child. "I think you are mis-remembering the name you saw."

"Something is very wrong here, Arthur," muttered Isaac, addressing the captain informally in his distress. "The Callaway travelled to New York, aye, but never arrived. She was lost at sea and never found."

"I am beginning to agree with you, Isaac. Something is indeed very wrong here. Rose," the captain said, softening his voice in an attempt to calm the girl as he addressed her. "I do not blame you for anything. The animals' deaths are not your fault."

"Liar! You believe I have cursed your ship, because I have red hair. You think I am a witch, or a demon, and I will bring you all death and destruction."

Rose took another step backwards. Oliver reached out and grabbed her by the arm to stop her from retreating further, but he snatched his hand away with a hiss of pain.

Oliver held up his hand for Arthur to see. The palm was red and blistered, as though the skin had been burned. "She's ice cold, Captain. Touching her is like placing my hand into a glacier."

Rose huddled into herself, wrapping her skinny arms around her middle. Her pale skin faded from its former porcelain complexion to a light blue; the shade of ice forming over a winter river. Her breath condensed in front of her in a cloud of foggy vapour.

"So c-c-cold," she stammered, shivering. "Will n-n-not let you send m-m-me away."

Arthur moved toward the girl. She skittered away from him, eyes wary and darting toward the other men to see if they would try to reach her as well. The captain stopped and held out one hand, palm out, to assure her he would not come any closer.

"Rose. Please tell me what happened on the Callaway."

The caution in her eyes disappeared, replaced in an instant by anger. Although her skin remained a frozen blue, her hair waved and roiled in a non-existent wind, forming a corona of fire that surrounded her head and shoulders.

"Storms plagued the ship and one of the screws failed, slowing us to little more than a crawl across the waves. When our supplies began to spoil, the men working on the ship looked for reasons to explain their bad luck. Looking for excuses. They wanted something they could control rather than admit their own fate was now out of their hands.

"They blamed me. They said my red hair was bringing them all ill luck. Some claimed I was a witch and my demon familiars were coming to claim the souls of all the men and women onboard the Callaway. The Captain was facing a riot, so did nothing to try to save me.

"I was taken from my mother's arms. She tried to

hold on to me, but the men threatened to throw her into the ocean with me if she interfered. My father grabbed my mother and held her as I was dragged away from her. He was a coward. He would do nothing to save me if it threatened his own safety. He could not even look in my direction as I screamed for assistance and escape. My father turned his back to me, leaving me to the attentions of the men who desired me dead and gone."

Rose raised an accusing finger. She pointed toward Oliver and his companion, then let her hand drift to indicate Isaac and Arthur. "Just as you all wish me dead."

"I was thrown over the railing and into the sea. Like garbage. With no more thought than you would give dumping your chamber pot. The freezing cold of the water shocked the air from my very lungs. I couldn't breathe, and my limbs became heavy and numb. I could not even muster enough breath to cry out. I watched as the ship moved away from me, leaving me behind. I remember every moment of it, now. The taste of salt in my mouth. The drag of the water in my dress, trying to pull me under.

"I also remember praying to God to punish them. Not for rescue, for I knew the merciless ocean had already done for me. My life would end in the cold and the dark of its depths. I knew that as surely as I knew, I hated every person aboard the Callaway to the core of my very heart and soul. Instead, I prayed for revenge. I wanted the men who threw me away to pay for their actions. I wanted the crew who stood by and did not attempt to stop their fellow black-hearts to suffer an agonising end. Even my mother and father were in my prayers for not fighting for me. Not hard enough to matter. Yet, God did not hear me.

"But something else did."

"You died, Rose?" asked Arthur. "Those men on the Callaway killed you, and you cursed them as you died."

"I died," she agreed. "The cold water claimed me. There was nothing I, a child of no consequence, could do to stop it. Now, you want to throw me aside, just as they did. Only this time, you are too late. I am strong enough to fight back. I will return to the cold—I always do—but I will not be alone when I go."

"I was never going to harm you, Rose."

She laughed at Arthur's words. She did not believe them.

"I want to visit that lovely warm room again," she said. "Just for a little while. It felt so nice there."

Rose sank into the bowels of the ship, lowering slowly through the wood and metal of the deck. There was no longer any reason for her to pretend she was just a normal little girl; no reason to heed the laws by which the living must abide.

When the last strands of her flaming hair disappeared, Arthur turned to face the prow of the boat, staring out at the view he had so recently considered to be a blessing. That calm sea would soon be their tomb.

Arthur wondered if he had thrown Rose from the ship when Isaac first found her. Could he have saved the Spector from its fate? Or perhaps sending her overboard would only have hastened their demise. There was no way to know. He could not take himself back in time to find out. There would never be an answer to that question.

Arthur was currently certain of only one thing: the Spector, like the Callaway before it, would never see New York.

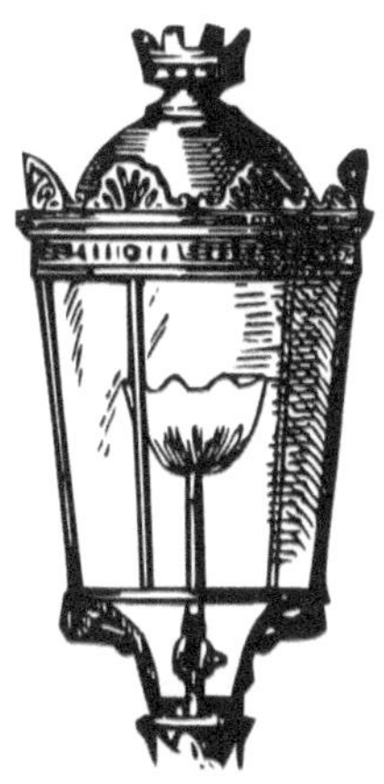

LAMPLIGHT

JONATHAN INBODY

"So what is it you're hoping to see?"

I turned to look at the small boat's captain, a middle-aged and persnickety man named Howie, then pulled my coat's collar tight around my neck as the cold ocean air rushed past us. "What do you mean?"

The salt-and-pepper haired man scratched the back of his neck. "Well, you're not a tourist or you'd have gone with one of the sight-seeing groups, but you didn't bring none of that fancy electrical equipment either, so you're not one of those... ghost hunters."

I smiled. "No, I'm not. I'm a historian; I'm working on a book of New England folk tales. It's turning into a kind of travelogue… My editor says those sell better."

"You oughta done one of those tours, then," Howie replied. "They'll give you all the spooky bells and ghostly whistles."

I shook my head. "That's not the part I'm interested in."

"You don't believe in ghosts?"

"Not really," I replied. "Either way, they don't scare me. As far as I can tell, they're not real, and if they were, then they couldn't hurt me, anyway. Besides, I don't want to hear the versions of the stories that get told to tourists; I've probably read them already. I want to know the stories that the locals tell each other, all the little details that don't catch a stranger's attention. And I want to see the places the stories sprang up from."

"Well, this one lives up to its reputation," Howie assured me. "Just seeing it in the dark sends a chill down my spine. Dangerous, too; that's why they don't like folks being out here late."

I looked out at the open bay in front of us, the dark blue water sitting below low-hanging clouds that seemed to almost glow in the quickly fading sunset. It was beautiful, in the way many places could have been, but eerie in a way that seemed exclusively New England. Already, I could see small clouds of thin fog rolling out over the rocky shoreline and onto the land, and the sea seemed almost unnaturally calm.

Somewhere out in front of us was Beckett Island, with the beached ship Lamplighter and the burned-out husk of an old stone lighthouse. It had long been known for strange balls of light that seemed to dance on the water, St. Elmo's fire or some weather condition much like it, and with the tragedy of the Lamplighter's grounding, the myths had only intensified. By the 1940s, the strange lights were said to be the spirits of the ship's long-dead crew, still holding their lanterns up to see through the fog.

It was quaint, the way ghost stories often are, but as we got further out of the bay and turned towards the darkening silhouette of Beckett Island, I had to admit the mood the townsfolk had set was strangely effective. While Howie circled the island and found us a place to go aground, I ran through the stories I had found in my research in my head.

"If the fog gets any thicker, we'll have to head back," Howie said, tying the boat in place on a rickety dock just down a small hill from the burned-out lighthouse. "Otherwise we could get stuck out here for the night."

"I'd really prefer to avoid that," I replied, hopping down from the boat and onto the island's rocky shore. I looked up the hill at the caved-in top of the crumbled lighthouse, then back at Howie. "So how did it happen?"

He followed my gaze to the lighthouse. "The fire, you mean? Haven't you heard the story?"

I smiled. "I want to hear it from you."

He shrugged, then hopped down from inside his boat and started up the hill, gesturing for me to follow. "Well, early on, long 'fore the lighthouse, this island was some kind of… religious place for the natives; somewhere to commune with the spirits of nature. And when they got pushed out, and shipping lines started running up and down the coast, well, the fog and the ghost lights started to do a number on a lot of ships."

"Ghost lights?"

"Yeah, that's what a lot of folks call 'em, anyways," Howie answered. "Either way, more than a few ships went down out here, so the city took up a vote and built a lighthouse. For a while, things were better, and then all at once they got a lot worse. A fire starts at the bottom of the lighthouse, burns up all the wood and makes the stone around it collapse; whole lamp fell right through to the bottom of the tower and shattered into a million little pieces."

"And that's when the Lamplighter came?" I asked, quickly typing notes on my phone.

He clicked his tongue, then cocked his head to one side. "Well, that's what a lot of folks say; Lamplighter came by, had no light to warn 'em off, ran aground onto the island… a lot of good sailors died."

I looked up from my notes. "But you don't think that's what happened?"

"Maybe it could be, but that's not the story the survivors told. The sailors that got fished out of the icy water, or pulled off of the rocks by the rescue boats, all of them that had been up on deck when it happened said the same thing; they could see the light shining, clear as day, and they changed course to steer around it only to smash right into the side of the island."

"But how is that possible?" I asked. "You can't point someone in the wrong direction with a lighthouse, the light is just a warning."

He chuckled. "That ain't the strangest part - by the time the ship came through, the lighthouse had already collapsed. All they found was a half-smashed tower of burning rock."

"It was a ghost light, then? The one that they saw?"

He nodded. "Must have been."

We stopped at the top of the hill and looked at the burned-out husk of the once-great stone lighthouse. Howie reached into his pocket and took out a long metal flashlight, then turned it on and ran the flashlight beam down the shoreline. I hadn't realised how dark it had gotten, but the heavy clouds above us seemed to snuff out even the barest shred of moonlight.

"The survivors, few though they were, huddled together around the burning lighthouse for warmth. They could hear sailors screaming for help off in the water, but with the fog… there was nothing to do but hope. Every now and again, they'd see a light shine somewhere off in the fog, sickly yellow like a dim lantern. They got in their heads that it was their drowned shipmates, trying to find their way to land even in death."

"But what about the lighthouse?" I asked. "How did the fire start?"

"Don't rightly know," he replied. "When the lens fell, it landed on the keeper; he was cut to ribbons by the glass, and what was left got burnt up and picked apart by seabirds before anyone thought to recover the body. Word is he went crazy, though. I guess he'd been talking about ghosts hiding in the fog, coming up to the door of the lighthouse and trying to get in… Wouldn't surprise me none if he started the fire himself, trying to scare off the spirits."

He leaned in, lowered his voice, and met my eyes. "Even though nobody is allowed out here at night anymore, people on shore say they can still see yellow lights dancing in the fog."

I smiled, and he let out a low chuckle. He seemed almost tickled by how well he had told the story, and more than that, how attentively I had listened.

I pointed at Howie's flashlight. "Do you mind?"

"Not at all," he replied, handing it over to me. "I've got another one in the boat; should've thought to bring it."

I cast the beam up from the shore and onto the collapsed lighthouse, taking in every detail visible in the charred brick. The flames had aged it, somehow, making it look more like an ancient ruin than a marvel of the last century. It had the authentic feel missing from so many of the typical haunted houses, aided by the genuine New England chill sweeping over the island and across the black water towards a cozy, formerly Colonial town.

"Is it safe to go aboard the ship?" I asked, turning back to Howie.

"I wouldn't risk it," he replied.

"I really think it'll help the piece."

He chuckled. "Why did you ask if you were going to do it, anyway?"

"I was hoping you'd say yes," I replied wryly.

I shined the flashlight across the length of the small island toward the crashed bulk of the Lamplighter. The metal behemoth sat crooked and tipped to one side on the rocky shore, with long streaks of crumpled and punctured metal on its bottom that looked like someone had taken a giant can opener to it. It, too, had more character than the average haunted house, with the rusted-out sheen of a bygone industrial era combined with the barnacle-ridden appearance of a subject of sea shanties.

I started walking down the hill towards it, glancing out at the foggy ocean surrounding us. Howie followed slowly behind me for a few steps, then stopped.

"I'll, uh…" he started nervously. "I'll go and get the other flashlight. You go on ahead."

"You don't have to come if you don't want to," I replied. "I only paid to use your boat."

A look of relief washed over his face and he nodded, then turned and started down the other side of the hill towards the rotted dock where we had tied off the ship. "Take as long as you like, but watch the fog. I'll call you back over if it gets thick enough that we have to turn back."

"Sure," I replied, turning back towards the Lamplighter. As I walked closer, another chill ran down my spine. It was amazing how effective ghost stories could be, especially in the dark, and thoughts of drowned sailors wandering through the fog by the dim light of their lanterns kept running through the back of my mind.

I stopped at the base of the tilted ship and reached up to grab the rusted railing, then stuck the flashlight in my coat's breast pocket and hoisted myself up, watching as the beam of light from the stowed flashlight danced awkwardly in the air above me. I swung my legs over the railing and dropped cautiously to the uneven deck, testing it to see if it would collapse under my weight. When it didn't, I began to slowly sidle along the slanted deck, holding both hands on the railing in front of me to keep from slipping.

It was difficult, moving without having the flashlight beam to guide me, but even pointing up into the open sky, the light did enough to light my immediate surroundings. With every breath I let out, I could see a small cloud of condensation float up and disappear into the black sky, and I shivered as I reached the Lamplighter's steerage cabin.

I tugged on the door, but it didn't budge. The wheel handle was rusted in place. I sighed and shimmied further to the next door on the side of the ship, one that was hanging ajar and rusted to the point of crumbling. Carefully positioning my hand in place on the railing, I reached up and took the flashlight from my coat pocket, then turned and shined the beam into the dark cabin beyond the hanging door.

All the furniture inside had slid against the wall and was mostly rotted, and at the far end of the room I could see another open door. I caught movement out of the corner of my eye and whipped the flashlight beam over to it, then sighed as a maroon coloured crab scuttled out of sight. The smell of salt was even stronger inside the rusted-out ship, and I remembered that the back end of the Lamplighter was still partially submerged. Was there water on the inside of the ship, too?

I pushed myself around the metal frame of the door and slid down into the room, holding a bolted-down metal table for stability as I scanned the next open door with the flashlight. I swore I could make out shapes in the pitch black, but what they were, I couldn't quite tell.

Suddenly, I saw a yellow glow at the edges of my vision, and the line around my shadow grew more defined as light shone into the black cabin from the doorway behind me.

For a long moment, I didn't move. I knew, deep down, that it must have been Howie, returned with an old lantern to try and scare me, but if I knew it, then why was I so afraid to turn and look? I could hear wet, heaving breaths getting closer by the second, and the light seemed to grow brighter as the plodding footsteps came to a stop just outside the open doorway. A tall shadow rose on the floor and dwarfed mine, and in a panic, I reached out and turned off the flashlight.

I stood frozen, holding myself steady on the bolted-down table and staring into the blackness of the room in front of me, waiting for the thing casting the shadow to move. The yellow glow seemed to wax and wane around me, almost flickering.

Ghosts aren't real, I repeated in my head, and if they are, they can't hurt me.

A trickle of water rolled down past my feet, and my breath caught in my throat. There was someone there, someone just behind me, someone soaked and dripping with a lit lantern held out in front of their head. They were breathing, gurgling really, like their lungs and throat had the waterlogged bloat of the drowned, and I could hear their weight shift and squeak on soggy boots.

Ghosts aren't real, and if they are, they can't hurt me.

The shadow shrank away, and the glow receded as soggy footsteps trailed off down the rusted deck of the ship, leaving me alone in the pitch-black cabin. I was trembling, almost shaking, and as I reached to turn the flashlight back on, I found myself dreading what I might see. I didn't believe in ghosts, not really, but I couldn't deny that whatever had been behind me felt less than human.

I slowly turned my head to look at the open doorway behind me, taking in two small puddles on the deck where two feet had just been. On the doorframe, too, was a wet patch from where a hand had just been resting. I could hear the soggy footsteps fading in the distance, and the yellow glow had all but gone.

I moved to reposition my legs and my shoe caught a slick patch, and before I knew it, I was tumbling down through the black doorway into the next cabin. I hit an overturned desk and rolled over it, then landed in six inches of icy water with an echoing splash.

I shined the flashlight around in the new room I had fallen into, then pulled myself up and out of the cold water. I was in a long, narrow room now, with metal tables that sat overturned or crookedly tipped, and from a doorway at the far end, I saw the eerie yellow glow of a distant light.

I clasped my hand over my mouth and pressed the front of the flashlight against my leg, snuffing out the beam except for an orange ring around its edge. Then, I heard the sound of wet footsteps again, slapping against distant metal and echoing from the far end of the long room across it to my ears. There was another one of the phantoms inside the ship, stirred awake by my fall. Was it looking for me? A long-dead sailor still roaming the halls of his ship in search of stowaways?

None of this was possible, was it? But I was seeing it with my own eyes, hearing phantom footsteps and hearing ghostly breaths. How could it be anything but real?

I scrambled up the slanted floor and pulled myself up through the doorway, staring forward at the doorway above me and the foggy sky beyond it as water trickled down the back of my clothes and began to pool in my shoes. I could see the yellow glow growing stronger around my feet as I pulled myself up through the next room and to the next doorway, and as I finally emerged onto the Lamplighter's deck I heard a low, terrible moan echo out from inside the ship.

I sidled down the slanted deck again, cautiously watching my wet shoes to make sure they weren't about to slip. My hands were shaking as they clutched the rusted railing, and I could feel my heartbeat pounding in my chest. The sky around me seemed almost overtaken by thick, white fog, and as I dropped down from the ship to the rocky shore, I realised I could no longer see the other side of the island, or the burnt-out lighthouse and rotted dock I knew were there.

I looked up at the derelict ship and shivered. I could see two faint yellow lights shining down from above, one far off at the ship's rear and one that seemed to be getting closer by the second. I turned and started running across the island, waving the flashlight out in front of me as I squinted into the fog.

"Howie!" I called out desperately, my voice breaking fearfully. "There's something out here with us!"

The lighthouse rose from inside the fog like an ancient, crumbled monolith, looming over me in black silhouette as I turned and splashed down through the mud covering the small hill leading to the dock. I knew now what had inspired such fear in the keeper, even without seeing it, and more than that I knew that if I let myself stop, even for a moment, his fate could be mine, too.

My soaked shoe slipped underneath me and I fell forward onto the rocky shore, then rolled and got back to my feet. I could make out the shape of Howie's ship, now, and his silhouette rising up in the cabin behind the wheel. I saw him reach up with one hand and scratch the back of his neck, leaning down to get a better look at me as I sprinted down the rotted dock towards him.

"Are you alright?" he called out. "What happened?"

I skidded to a stop, my voice catching in my throat as I opened my mouth to reply. Behind Howie's boat, a scattering of yellow lights seemed to dance in the fog, bobbing with the waves as the dark shapes inside them moved towards shore.

As I looked back at Howie, I saw one of the ghost lights shine into the cabin from the open door behind him. He whirled and the dark shape holding the light aloft leapt onto him, its lantern swinging back and forth as I heard him struggling and scream. I heard the tearing of flesh, a wet, nauseating rip, and watched a stream of hot blood splatter against the ship's cold window.

I took a terrified step back, then turned to look back at the fog-shrouded sea, now teeming with floating yellow lights. They were looking for me, coming for me, ready to drag me down beneath the waves and drown me like they had been drowned.

With a booming splash, a gigantic yellow light

rose up through the fog in the distance, then turned and shined down on my trembling form like Hell's spotlight. The shape underneath it was massive, but as I tried to make it out, my eyes went blind from the powerful light.

I stumbled forward, almost toppling off the rotted dock and into the salt-ridden sea, then looked up and saw a dark figure standing on the deck of Howie's ship as my vision came flooding back.

In the weeks since that night, I've tried to tell myself that what I saw was impossible, the panic-stricken hallucination of a man rendered temporarily insane. When they'd found me that morning on the mainland's shore, ranting and raving in Howie's blood covered boat, his mangled and slashed body sitting just next to my huddled form, they said I lost my mind. I had attacked him, they said, killed him. But I know what I saw.

I was right. God help me, I was right. What I saw that night was no ghost, no trick of the light or dispossessed soul of the damned. I had fought it off, by some miracle, and driven Howie's boat blindly into the fog, only to find myself back on shore by the same miraculous chance. But how could I tell them what it was out there that night in Beckett Bay? How could I make them believe me?

How could I make them understand that what I had seen was in the scale-covered, hunched-over shape of a man, but that the form itself was entirely different? The thing standing on the deck above me that night had the grotesque head and wide, jagged-toothed mouth of an anglerfish. And dangling down from above it, bobbing like a lantern held aloft in the fog, was a fleshy lure that flickered from within with a sickly yellow light.

LEVIATHAN

DALE PARNELL

The engine was dead, and the Megan drifted aimlessly as ink-black waves towered above us, smashing against the hull with deafening hammer blows. We were three days out of port when the storm hit, the worst I've seen in ten years fishing, and when the diesel engine spluttered and ground to a halt, each of us feared it would take a miracle to see us returned home safely.

The Skipper barked his orders, and we fought the wind and freezing spray to secure the Megan as best we could. The old girl complained loudly in the squall, pitching about blindly in the darkness, threatening to toss you overboard if she caught you unawares. The Skipper was a hard man, righteous and holy, and we knew it would take more than a mere storm, however brutal, to see his expectations of us eased even a little.

With everything tied down tightly, the crew retired to the mess, deep in the belly of the Megan, and the Skipper mercifully opened a bottle from his private reserve to try to settle our nerves. We spent that first hour in silence, the bottle being passed wordlessly from person to person as we listened to the howling wind build in strength, sounding like the unholy screams of the devil himself.

And just as we grew accustomed to the constant noise and rolling of the ship, the solitary lightbulb in the mess blinked out, plunging the small, tense space into instant darkness. There were scuffles and muttered curses as men clambered over each other to escape the claustrophobic room until the Skipper's strong voice finally cut through the panic and set us to work.

He sent me to the engine room, along with Jones and Peterson, to find out what had happened, whilst the others he ordered to check the cabins and deck. The Skipper himself headed for the wheelhouse to make sure none of the vital instruments had shorted out.

I followed Jones along the narrow passageway to the hatch leading down into the engine room, Peterson trailing behind, each of us feeling our way through the ship, counting off doorways and junction boxes to keep track of our position. We made our way quickly from the mess to the engine room down pitch-black corridors, the sound of the wind and waves beating down angrily on the deck above our heads.

Once in the low-ceiled engine room, Peterson

quickly put his hand to a lamp, and we set about checking the generator. The gauges were frozen in place, and we discovered the thick rubber wire leading away scorched and melted around the connection points. Peterson confirmed he could fix it if a replacement cable could be found. We searched the repair lockers only to come away empty-handed and Peterson thought a while before stating that he would have to salvage a length of cable from somewhere on board, and he and Jones set off with the lamp to search for a suitable donor.

I paused a while in the engine room, the silence and dark seeming so alien in a room I had only ever seen thrumming with light and sound, thinking that I would wait for Jones and Peterson to return, when a sudden, ear-splitting scream from up on deck made me flinch in terror. The scream was followed a few moments later by cursing and hollering, the likes of which would have put Bedlam to shame. And finally, finding my courage, I dashed across the engine room to the ladder leading straight up to the open deck.

Emerging in the dark, salty air, I was instantly battered by tremendous gales sweeping back and forth across the ship, and I struggled to secure a strong grip on the sodden railings. Pulling myself along the starboard runway, trying to shield my eyes from the stinging rain, I spied the Skipper standing outside the wheelhouse up above me, one hand wrapped around the thin railing, the other clutching tightly to a spent flare-gun. I called out to him as loudly as I could, my small voice insignificant against the maelstrom that was bearing down on us, and so I crawled my way along, fighting up the short ladder to stand beside him on the upper deck.

"What is it?" I screamed, holding my face close to his.

"There!" he bellowed, his eyes wild and staring as he pointed up and out towards the huge, black waves that dwarfed our stricken ship.

I followed his gaze, squinting into the darkness, seeing nothing but an empty void out beyond the prow of the Megan. The bullet-hard rain lashed at my face and I feared that the Skipper had cracked, but then I saw it; a fleeting, haunting glimpse of something huge and terrible that flashed through the dark water. I turned to the Skipper to find him staring wide-eyed at me.

"You saw it. You saw it!" he screamed; his voice laden with manic vindication.

"We have to go!" I shouted, pointing down below decks. The Skipper nodded, a strange, glassy look settling upon his weathered face. And together we climbed down from the deck and returned to the mess.

In the chattering, still darkness, the Skipper remained silent, a mercy I was thankful for, and we waited until finally the single, yellowed bulb hanging loosely from the ceiling flickered to life, the cheers from the crew accompanied by the low, droning buzz of the restored generator. In a short time, Jones and Peterson returned to a chorus of grateful backslaps and warm embraces. The storm outside continued to rage, but I was grateful for the change of mood, and for a moment I believed it may be enough to see us through the night. But as the chatter died down, the Skipper, sitting alone in a far corner of the room, finally spoke up, his voice low and ominous.

"The storm has woken a beast," he said, holding each crewmate's gaze in turn. "It will sink us for sure."

A few laughed uncertainly, looking about the room for reassurance, whilst others looked up towards the deck, cocking their heads to listen to the wind and rain and ocean churning about us.

"It is a leviathan," the Skipper continued, standing from his seat and pacing around the small room. "The seabed has split open and the demons of hell have been freed."

The nervous laughter ceased, and worried faces began turning to each other.

"It cannot be true?" Peterson asked, turning to me for an answer I could not give.

"We must kill it," the Skipper said firmly. And in a blur of movement, he was away, disappearing from the mess at a sprint, leaving behind mutterings and fearful questions. I looked to Peterson and Sawyer, the largest and strongest of the crew, and urged them to follow me after the Skipper.

We emerged onto the deck, the pitch and roll of the ship giving a true test of our sea legs, and staring about the ship, the sky suddenly erupted with a brilliant white flash of lightning, followed closely by a deep bass rumbling that I felt deep in my skull. Sawyer's voice, almost drowned out by the wind, caught my attention, and turning I saw him point to the stern of the ship, where the Skipper stood proud, the longest and sturdiest of our boat hooks held firmly in his grasp as a hunter would wield a spear. Before we could act, the Skipper fired a flare, the arcing red flame casting its light weakly over the black sky and waters.

But it was enough to see by.

Before us stood the sheer cliff-face of a mighty wave, its top-most edge lost in the dark clouds that now hung low above us, smothering the sky. And across the face of the wave it swam, larger than any ship or whale that I have ever seen or heard tell of, its oily hide shimmering like quicksilver. I could not describe its form, for in truth it was too strange and terrifying for my mind to take in, and in that moment I was nothing but a helpless infant, wishing for a mother's arms to come sweep me away.

We stared dumbfounded, watching as the creature circled the ship before disappearing into the black waters beneath us. Our stupefied minds were brought back by the sudden roaring cry that came forth from the Skipper, as he railed and cursed the sky and the waves, his rain swollen hands fumbling to load a fresh flare. Coming to my senses, I broke into a run, tearing across the deck, fighting with gritted teeth against the fierce wind that tried to hold me back. Sawyer and Peterson shook off their own paralysis and ran to join me, and we reached the Skipper together. He would not hear our cries to retreat, and I could see from his glazed expression that mania had taken him completely. Seizing his arms, I struggled to hold him, and seeing my plan, Sawyer joined me, and we wrestled the Skipper to the deck as Peterson went for a length of rope from a nearby locker.

As we tied him down, the Skipper's ranting grew more ferocious, his body seemingly possessed of an unnatural strength, his voice roaring high above the piercing wind and rain. I gagged his mouth, fearful that his curses would drive the rest of the crew mad along with him, and we three continued to lash him in place to the railings. When at last it was done, we stepped back uncertainly, and I spied Peterson mouth a short, silent prayer. Mutiny is not a thing to be undertaken lightly, no matter the circumstances, and the responsibility sat heavily on our shoulders. Looking up slowly, I peered into the Skipper's ashen face, and at the sight of his eyes, my blood ran cold. Turning suddenly, I saw it too. The Skipper's wild screaming had finally caught the beast's attention, and its terrible body hung wetly above us.

I cannot say how I knew, for how could I have seen anything clearly through the thick blanket of rain and the low, black clouds that stood barely above our shoulders, but I knew without question that the thing had fixed its cold, dead stare on us. Lesser creatures know when they are being hunted; some ancient, primitive part of the brain senses the danger, and the body is flooded with adrenaline, urging you to run and hide. But what could we do? We were lost in a storm that had been raging since the beginning of time. The beast had always been hunting us, waiting in the depths of the cold ocean for its chance to feed. To either side of me, Peterson and Sawyer fell to their knees, curling themselves up and babbling like newborn babes waiting to be suckled. The Skipper sat frozen, unable to look away, his madness now total and complete. And me, standing alone on deck as the furious ocean toyed with us. Sailors and fishermen often talk of the sea as a mistress, lusty and demanding. But on this night she was a Queen, heartless and raving, and growing tired of her games she has set loose her dogs, bloody and furious, to end things.

The sky flashed a brilliant white, illuminating the world for all who dared to see, but I held tight my eyes, refusing to see any more. And as the low, gut-wrenching rumble of the clouds assaulted my ears, I felt the air around me stir as the creature struck, its monstrous jaws agape and hungry.

I do not know how long the storm raged, or what became of the Megan and her crew. I only know that I awoke, half drowned and half mad, my body washed ashore thirty miles east of our port.

A lone fisherman found me sometime later that morning as he climbed the beach, his homemade lobster pots slung over one shoulder. For anyone who has spent their life at sea, there is a look you see on certain men's faces that can never be forgotten. The fisherman spied me from a distance and approaching slowly; he seemed at once to understand. Wordlessly, he helped me to my feet and guided me patiently to his car beyond the low dunes. We drove the short distance to the nearest village in silence, and he banged on the door of the local public house until the landlord let us in, furnishing me with a large brandy before disappearing to telephone the authorities.

The fisherman set to work building a fire in the hearth, and once it was lit, he sat back, watching the flames.

"The storm?" the fisherman asked, his voice low

and gruff.

"Aye," I managed, my body shivering. "But there was…" I tried to find the words, but nothing more would come.

The fisherman stayed quiet for a while, and gradually I began to feel the warmth from the fire seep into my bones a little.

"How many?" the fisherman asked eventually, turning a little to face me.

"Eight souls," I replied, my voice catching in my throat, and I sank the remainder of the brandy in one gulp.

"At least you survived," the fisherman said finally. "That's something."

"Aye, that's something," I replied, tears and saltwater running freely and soaking into the carpet at my feet, as outside the window, bilious, flint-coloured clouds rolled out beyond the horizon.

THE CURSE OF THE PROTEUS

MARK RANKIN

I write the following to serve as a warning to all who may come across this doomed vessel. So that posterity will have a record of the evil unleashed upon the honest, seafaring men of the good ship Dauntless. I know not the hour, nor even the day, for time has lost all meaning to me. A great madness descended upon this vessel. A madness that left us becalmed in the middle of the bitterest storm, at the cost of twelve good lives. An insanity which will doubtless claim one more soul before this night is done.

I can feel the winds as they fill the sails once more, and I can hear the creak of the timbers beneath the cabin as the ocean currents move us. But it is too late. The candle burning on the table beside me will be the last light my living eyes will see. I can only pray to all that is holy, that I will have time enough to tell my tale before it gutters and dies.

But where to start? Do I tell you of the bright, cool autumn day we left The Port of London, the hold of the good ship Dauntless laden with a cargo of silk, linen, and wool and provisions generous enough to sate the hunger and thirst of all thirteen souls who climbed the gangplank that morn? How we raised anchor and set sail to the new world hale, hearty, and boisterous of mood? Do I tell of the sixteen days spent navigating the mighty Germanic Sea in a vessel not two years of age, a fair wind and a following sea to aid our passage? No, I shall not dwell on the details of those halcyon days of hard work and high spirits. It is enough to state that when the sky first darkened, and we sighted the bones of the merchant brig Proteus on the horizon, we were, to a man, blessed with health, happy camaraderie, and a universal thirst for some small adventure with which to break the monotony of our journey. A wish soon to be granted in the most horrific of circumstances.

"Ship-Ho!"

The shout came from above us in the crackled, high-pitched tones of Simeon Fields. The youngest member of the crew at just seventeen years of age, the coltish youth was at his customary post high in the ship's rigging, his sandy hair blowing, and his eye trained on the horizon. At his words, his brother, Benedict, three years his senior, but experienced even beyond that, raced to the port bow, one hand resting on his brow as if to help him see the vessel his sibling had spotted.

"It's another brig, Mister Emery!" He shouted over his shoulder.

Prompted by the assertion, I took out my Dollond and raised it to my eye. The elder Field had not erred. The twin, square-rigged masts were a testament to that. What he had failed to mention, or perhaps failed to spy, was one of those masts leaned to one side at an alarming angle, the sails it supported hanging like a bedsheet upon a housemaid's line. I let my glass move down towards the prow where the figurehead of a crowned and muscular man with a short, thick beard not unlike my own.

The grim-faced sea-God held forth a double-ended trident, three curved points sitting atop its haft and straight, downward pointing, tines at its lower end. This grim effigy's lower half, a serpent's tail, stood upon a nameplate which declared the identity of both figurehead and ship as Proteus. On the deck and in the rigging, there was not one sign of life. No crewmen to right the rigging, no captain or mate to bellow instructions. Nothing. The injured ship was as becalmed on deck as it was below, and just as rudderless, too. I tapped the Dollond to my lip as I gave the ship some thought. If the decision had been mine, the matter would be simple. A stricken vessel lay within reach, with the chance that injured men may be aboard, and the code of the sea said if help were needed then that help should be offered. As First Mate, the decision was not mine to make, however.

That honour fell to the ship's Master. And with the risk of heading into a gathering storm, and the time lost as a result. Captain Samuel Blethyn could not be relied upon to reach the same conclusion. I formed a loose plan, turned aftwards, and made ready to summon my captain from his cabin. My task proved to be a redundant one.

"Mr Emery, what is the cause for this unseemly alarm?" Captain Blethyn strode toward me, pulling smooth his shirt-front over his stomach and straightening his tricorne as he neared. From the glaze of his eye, and the rum on his breath, it was plain the man had taken to his bed for some rest, and also that he had taken with him his habitual aid to restless slumber, too.

"A ship, Captain." The elder Field replied before I had time to form my words. "Stricken, and without our aid, surely doomed to the ocean floor."

The captain, a fellow of advancing years, and worsening temper, favoured the man with a glare which would have frozen the blood of a less hardy soul and reached a hand out toward me. I answered his unspoken request with a bow of the head and the proffering of my trusty 'scope which Blethyn put to his eye. "Aye," he muttered. "So it would appear. But at what delay would that aid be proffered? And at what cost to our enterprise?"

It was upon hearing these words I made the intervention which will forever haunt me, be it in this life or the next. A few simple words, spoken quietly, but with full knowledge of the strength they held. Words I knew Samuel Blethyn would be powerless against.

"The ship is a merchant brig, and it would appear laden, Captain. Laden and seemingly deserted."

Blethyn took the Dollond to his eye again to check on my assertions. It would be easy for a man of his experience to see the way the unsteady vessel lay so low and heavy upon the waves. Easy for him to surmise, as I had before him, that this meant a heavy cargo waited in its hold.

"Deserted?"

"There may be men below deck." The younger Field jumped the last four feet from the rigging and stood by his brother. From the aft of the ship and from below deck, the rest of the crew gathered; drawn by the excitement. "But if so, then they must surely lie injured or suffering from some malady. No sailor of sound body and mind would leave a ship to list in such a fashion."

The captain's head bobbed in a slow, thoughtful cadence as he considered the crewman's words. "Aye, and if that be the case, it would not befit us to add to their peril. Mr Emery, make ready the ship's boat. When we near our stricken brothers-at-sea, take three men of your choosing and let us see what help we may provide and what, if anything, we may salvage from this tragedy."

I bowed my head, gestured to Benedict Field, Elias Ford, the ship's carpenter, and able seaman Franklin Carlisle, and together, the four of us made ready to do as our captain bade.

The ship's boat, called by some a Pinnace, was more than large enough for our meagre crew, and with Franklin Carlisle, a giant of a man by any estimation, manning the tiller and the keen-eyed Benedict Field keeping a close watch on the small sail, we were soon arrowing through the waves. Above our heads, clouds gathered, black as eternal sin, and filled with the promise of a dire storm. The air felt heavy, the licks of brine that flew up from the ocean's surface to pepper our faces the only relief from the oppressive atmosphere. It was Elias Ford who punctured this pensive silence, as he let loose a frantic alarm.

"What the devil? Mr Emery, look yonder."

He pointed at the ship we thought abandoned. There, leaning against the ship's rail, was the figure of a man. He stood tall, a woolen jacket covering his blood-stained white shirt. Atop his head perched a red cap from under which blonde hair streamed onto his shoulders. I raised my hand in greeting, hoping to capture the man's attention, but to my dismay he turned and marched from view.

"I thought the vessel forsaken?" The glance Ford threw my way brimmed with dire misgiving and not a little suspicion. "That is what you told the captain, is it not?"

"Then it would appear I spoke in error." I kept my eyes on the rail. "A fortuitous error if the blood on our friend's shirt is any clue, for I doubt our captain would have spared his men for any venture which may carry the risk of confrontation, but an error all the same. Now make ready the hooks. We will soon be within range to board, and see what assistance we may provide."

The men shared a nervous glance, which travelled around the boat. They were a hardy bunch, thick of sinew and calloused of hand. Men who had faced down the heaviest of storms and the wildest of seas. Men who had risked their lives again and again and again until the risk was an ally they sought. But still, something about The

Proteus unnerved these hardy sailors. And I could feel it too. A visceral chill that had nothing to do with the closing storm chased down my spine and throughout each limb. An icy finger of dread. Not fear. Dread. A hopeless, helpless sense of an approaching and inevitable doom that lay cold and heavy upon my heart. I looked once more at our destination, the ship which lay so still on the heaving waters. Its timbers dark, its sails torn and ragged. An invisible cloud of salty sourness and burnt ozone hung over the vessel like a shroud, and the smell of decay was everywhere about us. Underneath the gathering storm, the Proteus made for an imposing sight, but it was, after all, nothing but a half-wrecked ship. A thing of wood, and metal, and canvas, and rope. There was nothing to fear here. Such fancies belonged to the wildest tales of the ocean. To The Flying Dutchman, to The Marie Celeste. I shook my head to clear it, and barked out a series of orders in the hope I could do the same for my men.

"Mr Carlisle! Mr Field! The ropes! Now! Mr Ford make the boat safe and ensure each man is armed, I care not with what." I took out my pistol and made it ready to fire, my actions designed to spread confidence and thoughts of security among my small crew.

The men made themselves busy and within the space of a few minutes, a pair of grappling hooks were sailing through the air toward the rail of the good ship Proteus.

I had not thought to bring a lantern with us, it being but early afternoon, but as Franklin Carlisle helped Benedict Field over the ship's rail, I wished with all my heart I had. The sky had once again darkened. Sullen black and bruised purple clouds covered the sky, blocking out the sun's rays. It was as if a great storm gathered above us but refused to break. Held in some strange stasis by inhuman hands. Lending the very air around us a still, oppressive texture. The men gathered around me, their weight shifting from foot to foot as each looked around them at the ruin of what had once been a proud and noble vessel.

What remained was a true wreck. The timbers warped until the surface we stood on cambered in strange and contradictory ways. One portion of the deck, off to-ward the fo'c's'le, blackened, as if by a great fire. The rigging, a spider's web of confusion, joined here and there by thick strands of something darkly shining and gelatinous.

"What has happened here?" Field's face was ashen, his eyes wild.

"It is the devil's work." Franklin Carlisle pulled a small cross from beneath his shirt and held it before him, its short chain allowing it to be raised to the level of his mouth. "This is an unholy place, Mr Emery. We should leave. Now. Leave and never return."

I looked across to Elias Ford. The ship's carpenter still glared at me with distrust and menace. His eyes as dark as his raven-wing hair.

"Not before we accomplish what we came here for." I took a step back and let my gaze travel from man to man. "We search the ship. We find the man we saw earli-er, and any crewmates which may remain…"

"And any valuables the captain may see fit to reward us for." Ford's voice was low. His eyes still fixed on me. "Let us not forget that."

"We search the ship? You mean we go below deck?" Benedict Field's tone told me he found the notion less than enticing.

"I do. We go together, we move fast, and we keep our wits about us, and our weapons handy. We are men of the sea and although we may prepare ourselves against the threat of the unknown, we will not allow ourselves to be cowed by petty superstitions. Any survivors, or any salvage worth taking…" I shot Ford a glance. "…we take back to The Dauntless. After that, it is for the captain to decide on what happens. Now I suggest we get our worthless arses moving before words are spilled that cannot be taken back."

A shallow flight of steps led down into the belly of the boat and the crew's quarters. At their end hung a lantern, which Elias Ford took out his flint and lit.

A narrow table, five feet long and two wide, hung from the low ceiling. On either side of it stood equally narrow benches. Against the wall to our left, a pair of shorter benches stood beneath a half-dozen hammocks, two deployed and the rest folded and waiting for use. In the right-hand corner of the squat room sat the ship's stove. It painted a picture of a crew similar in number and make-up to our own, but it painted so much more, too.

There were no bodies, but it was clear people had

died here. The blood stains on the walls, the floor, and the long streak which ran from a dagger impaled in the surface of the suspended table onto the boards beneath told that much. It was too much blood for one person, and when the scorch marks decorating the far wall, and the tin plates, tankards, and food waste on the floor were taken into account, it told a tale of a frantic struggle to the death, but a struggle with what? That was the question. Had the men who supped here settled a disagreement with small arms, blades and flying fists or had they banded together against a common enemy?

We spread out in the room, each of us examining the space around us. Elias Ford ran his hand over the surface of the table and up over the handle of the knife. A quick tug pulled it free, and he brought it up to his eyes, watching the dim light glint along the blade. Satisfied, he ended his examination, took a surreptitious glance around and slipped it into his pocket. Then he turned his attention elsewhere.

"There's more of that black stuff." Ford stared aghast at a portion of the wall where it joined the timbers of the deck above.

There the varnished wood was stained with the same dark and viscous gunk evident earlier. A casual observer might conjecture that it had oozed down from the deck, seeking every crack and crevice in order to infiltrate the ship's interior, but any vessel made good against the sea and the elements should prove hardier still against something so viscous. Besides which, from the pattern of the material's flow, it had not dripped down but somehow made its way up the wall, as if to seek the freedom of the briny air. A sight both uncanny and abhorrent, and one that churned my stomach worse than any storm I've sailed through in ten years or more.

"What is it?" Franklin Carlisle came to Ford's shoulder, his gaze following to where the shorter man stared. He reached up one sinewy arm, his height and great reach allowing him to touch the tar-like substance. With a shouted curse, he recoiled back, snatching his hand away as if scalded.

"Hellfire, man!" Field joined his crewmates and grabbed the giant's hand to examine it.

"Wait, there is no mark. No burn."

"Don't you think I know that?" Carlisle snatched his hand back. "Whatever this substance may be, it is not hot or abrasive."

"Cold then?" I joined the men and looked around me. We were alone in the galley, but it was feeling less and less so.

"No, not cold. Not in the way you mean, anyway. It just… I felt cold, but not here." He held out his hand. "I felt cold here." He tapped his chest. "Inside. Empty. A dead thing. It was as if everything that belongs to me, everything I am, was stripped from me by unseen hands, and I was left alone and abandoned on some desolate shore. A castaway, separated from all that is vital and alive by a great dark sea."

"But you touched it for only a second." Field's brow drew down even further.

"It felt longer. It still does."

A moment passed in which all was silence. The four of us gathered together in oppressive stillness, sharing uncertain glances filled with heavy unease.

"We need to leave this place." Field's words erupted from him in a garbled mess, shattering the silence.

The men nodded their agreement, and I made to speak mine, but a flash of white froze the words in my throat. An all too familiar male figure with blonde hair and a blood-soaked shirt passed the door by the side of the stove and turned to the stairs which led further down into the ship. The white of the cotton and the red of his cap leaving a fleeting yet indelible chill within my heart as the figure moved on in dead silence. I staggered back, falling heavily into the still stunned Franklin Carlisle, one raised arm stretching toward the doorway.

"Mr Emery?"

"There was someone at the doorway." I turned to look at Field. "Someone making for the hold."

"The hold?" Ford's voice dripped with sarcasm. "But what a coincidence. Is that not what we came here for? To liberate the valuables this vessel holds."

"And to save any souls on board." I reminded him.

"Souls, aye." Carlisle's eyes moved back to the unctuous mass on the wall. "If souls there be."

I did not answer Carlisle with words, but took the lantern from Ford and strode to the doorway. Only once there, with the light spilling into the darkness, did I turn and address my small crew. "There is only one way to find out. One way to discover if what I saw was reality or some trick of perception. One way to leave this place and whatever ails it with a clean conscience. We must descend."

"Aye!" Ford shouted. "Mr Emery is right. We must

go on." Without a glance back, he came to my side and, with a reluctance that was palpable, Carlisle and Field followed. Together we made our way down the wooden stairs, a pool of artificial light our guide.

Here the space was even more cramped. A narrow walkway led forward to cleave the space between crates piled to shoulder height, the pale wood stained dark green by age and decay. The air around them hung heavy with a dark and cloying scent. We could only traverse the cramped space in single file. I took the lead. Carlisle to the rear with Ford and Field sandwiched in between.

"Well, the ship wasn't carrying textiles." Field gestured at the rotting wood. "There'd be no need to box up bolts of silk or cotton. Those you'd just lay on tarpaulin and make sure they're well covered."

I let my head bob out a long, thoughtful rhythm as I searched the shadows, looking for the specter I had seen above. I raised the lantern high and swung it out both to port and starboard, but there was not one sign. Or so I thought.

"By all that is holy! Look there!" Ford cried. Pointing at a gap between the remnants of two crates.

I let the lamplight follow the sailor's finger and saw what he had pointed out. Propped up against the smashed wood was a skeleton, laid in an ungainly position, its meagre weight leaning to its left, its head resting on the opposite shoulder. The ribcage of the corpse poked out from tattered vestiges of a white cotton shirt and grimy blue jacket, all three pierced by a rusting blade. Atop the skull, a red cap perched, still in remarkably good condition. It looked very much like I had found my mysterious figure, or at least the remains of him.

"I think Mr Carlise was right. I think we should every one of us leave this place, and leave it now." The words felt heavy to me, almost as if they did not wish to be spoken, but I could see Franklin Carlisle nodding his enthusiastic agreement before I was halfway through them. Beside him, in the stunned expression of Benedict Field I saw the same sentiment echoed deep within his eyes. Elias Ford looked away from me. His eyes searching the ruined boxes with a strange hunger. I turned to make some remark to the man, but as I turned the light toward him, Field cried out.

"Mr Emery, the skeleton, it's holding something."

I turned the light back and saw what Field had spotted. As it moved the lamp's glow had reflected off the corner of a silver box, half covered in the leg bones of the corpse and the half-eaten scraps of white cotton trousers.

"Spoils for the captain!" Elias Ford didn't wait for either order of approval but dived over the crates which stood between him and his prize. Some shattered beneath his feet, others he knocked aside, and from all the sweet, noisome stench of rotten fruit escaped, as green mould and maggots spilled onto the floor. Ford ignored them, even as he slipped and one hand touched the writhing mass of corruption. With the other hand, he reached out and took hold of the silver box. It took the combined might of myself and Franklin Carlisle to drag him free.

"Hellfire man, what are you thinking?" The admonishment came from Benedict Field. "There could have been anything hiding in that pile of decay. Rats, venomous spiders of the Caribbean isles stowed aboard with the fruit, anything."

Carlisle raised the silver box, which measured perhaps two feet by one above his head and grinned, a strange sheen glazing his dark eyes. "Aye, perhaps, but I have my prize." Those too-bright eyes flashed my way. "For the captain, that is."

I might have made some reply. Might even have taken some action over the man's intemperate behaviour, but it was at that moment the ship listed. A mighty groan sounded and we fell against the rotting cargo of the Proteus as timbers moved against each other in torturous fashion and the starboard side of the ship fell. No words were necessary. No commands. No orders. To a man, we righted ourselves and made for the stairs with as much speed as we could muster and fled the hold, making our way past the crew's quarters and out into the acrid air of the still-threatening storm. A few drops of rain dampened the air, and as we reached the deck, a mighty wind moved through the stillness for the first time. The mast, which I had first seen half-collapsed through my glass, creaked one last time and began a slow and oddly graceful descent. As it crashed into the boards, it created a great hole and, for a moment, I feared the ship might drag us back below deck, but our speed was sufficient for all four of us to reach the side of the ship and clamber down into the small boat we had arrived on. The ropes untied and left behind, we pushed away from the Proteus as it collapsed in on itself, a great wave caused by its plunge beneath the waves aiding us in our escape. As Franklin Carlisle grabbed hold of the oars and Benedict Field went to aid him, we moved further and further from the shadow of the ship, until, content in our safety, I could turn and watch the roiling waves swallow the stricken brig Proteus whole.

"Mr Emery!" The captain rushed forward; his arms outstretched. To prepare for our return he had dressed himself in a more complete and dignified manner, and a naval-blue jacket with brass buttons covered the white of his shirt. "Mr Emery, thank the Lord you have returned to us. We saw the ship, breached and floundering and feared for our shipmates' lives."

I gave my superior officer the briefest of smiles, content in my surety that any fears the man had would have been constrained to the practicalities of sailing shorthanded and the time which we might lose as a result. In the periphery of my vision, I saw members of the crew offering more heartfelt greetings of relief and fellowship to the others in our party. Simeon Field flew to his brother and clasped him in a bear-hug filled with unspoken emotions.

"We return a full complement, my captain. Shaken, but unharmed." I stood to attention as I made my report. "The ship's demise granted us sufficient warning that we made our escape in the very nick of time, but make it we did."

"And regarding the purpose for your adventure?" Samuel Blethyn's eye twinkled in a way which forced me to recall the way Elias Ford had looked at me in the hold of the Proteus. A look which still left a discordant note of unease deep within me.

"We found no survivors on board." I knew this was not the captain's question but nevertheless, it was the one I chose to answer. "Myself and Mr Ford thought we saw someone, but that, I believe, was due to the unhealthy atmosphere which surrounded the vessel. Perhaps the rotting wood, or the putrescent fruit in the hold released something into the air which caused a temporary sickness."

Captain Blethyn assumed a thoughtful expression. His brow furrowed, and his lips pursed as he pretended to give this due consideration. "Perhaps so," he muttered, "perhaps so. But what of the other aim? What of the cargo and the valuables which we might save from the ocean's depths? Surely there was something salvageable from this terrible tragedy?"

"Mr Ford." I shouted the words over one shoulder, my eyes never leaving the captain's. "Front and centre, if you please. Bring the salvage with you."

Elias Ford extricated himself from his crew mates and approached us, his steps heavy, his face as dark as the thick clouds crowding the sky above. He drew to my side and thrust the silver box into my hands. "Mr Mate." He clipped a salute. "Just remember who risked their lives for this. Remember who deserves his fair share."

"It shall not be forgotten." Captain Blethyn extended his hand, and I placed the silver box on his palm. "No shall the efforts of any man." He took a knife from his belt and inserted the blade in the small gap betwixt the lid and the body of the small casket and prized it open. Inside were a collection of gold and silver coins, each larger than a crown by at least half, loose gemstone in a range of colours and cuts, and three or four pieces of jewelry shaped and crafted by hands as skilled as any I'd seen.

"I shall hold this in my cabin, under lock and key, until we reach shore. Then, and only then, will we look to share the spoils in the fairest and most equitable manner."

"Just as long as you remember who brought it to you," Ford snarled. I turned to stand in front of the ship's carpenter, and with nothing but a hard look, dismissed him back to his shipmates. The dark-haired man slouched away in a palpable cloud of misery.

"Thank you, Mr Emery." Captain Blethyn watched the unhappy man depart. "I expect that man to be dealt with. And if any others have brought back with them such an attitude, then I expect them to be dealt with, too." Holding the silver chest close to him, the captain turned on his heels and headed back to his cabin, leaving me to the companionship of my crewmates. A companionship that was soon to be ripped to shreds.

I cannot be sure if it was the next day or the day after that the ordeal started. As I mentioned, time had become stretched and torn in such a multitude of ways that I no longer know for certain how long we have been here. All I do remember is being called from my bunk by harsh shouts of dismay. Upon reaching the deck of the

Dauntless, I soon discovered the reason for such cries of distress. The sky was dark. Not the star-strewn darkness of night, but a close, almost solid darkness caused by a low cloud and a rising fog. No sun or moon was visible and not a lick of wind blew to disturb the grim miasma. It was more than that, however. There was a difference to the ship itself, one unmistakable to any man who had spent time at sea. We were still. Unmistakably and perfectly still. It wasn't just the air which had become becalmed but the ocean itself. The roll and heave that accompanies any sea-going vessel's passage, and which becomes such a feature of every sailor's life that it oft goes unnoticed, had disappeared. It was as if the sea and all the elements had become frozen, and us along with them.

"Mr Emery!" Simeon Field raced to me. His boyish face, so like that of his brother in so many ways, drip-white. "Mr Emery, we are so still. There is not a wisp of breeze and the ocean itself is like some dark mirror. Look!" He pointed to the rail and I strode over to gaze down at the waters below us. Sure enough, the surface of the mighty Northern Ocean was as quiet as a mill-pond. Not one wave disturbed its surface, not one ripple. The water, such a murky blend of darkest grey in the best of seasons, had distilled and clarified to a black sheen that reflected the heavy sky as if we were contained in a sphere of a glowering cloud. As the younger Field had said, it was like peering into the depths of some demonic looking glass.

"There's more, too," Benedict Field called from his brother's shoulder, interrupting my study of the unnatural storm of quietude we appeared to be trapped within. "The ship's boat is missing, and along with it, five hands."

"Has this news reached the captain?"

"No, sir. The captain cannot be roused. His cabin is locked, the door strong and stout, and neither the cries of the men, nor my own efforts have been enough to get him to open his door."

My eyes narrowed as I considered Field's words. If the captain had taken ill, or some misadventure had come upon him, it would be I who would lead the crew through this ordeal, I who would be responsible for the safety of both body and soul. My mind flew back to our encounter with the doomed ship Proteus. Was it possible we had brought back something of that cursed vessel with us? Or could our predicaments be symptoms of some joint fate? Could the same force which had stricken the vessel in such a calamitous fashion have now taken a hold on us? "Bring me some men, and something with which to break down that door, Mr Field. We will gain entry, ascertain the captain's circumstances and offer what aid is needed, then and only then, will we investigate those scurvy deserters and their reason for abandoning ship. Then we will form a plan to get us away from these accursed waters."

Field replied with a curt nod and shot off, his brother by his side. The elder Field barked orders at the first able seamen he could find and the younger assisted with emphatic gesticulations and his own yelped instructions. Content to leave them to their task, I strode to the door of the Master's cabin and waited for my aid to arrive.

Within the space of a few minutes, striding through the mist, both Fields returned with Franklin Carlise, Elias Ford, and abble seaman William Waterstone, a man who almost rivalled Carlisle in his imposing physicality.. Between Waterstone and Carlisle was slung a cooking pot, stolen from the galley, the pig iron pot some two-foot tall and half again as wide.

"My apologies, Mr Emery," Benedict Field said. "The cooking pot was all we could find with some weight to it, but between us I believe we have gathered muscle and sinew enough to break down any door, even be they the doors of hell itself."

I glanced round at the bleak, still surroundings. The air hung so heavy as to crush down upon me and carried with it that same acrid scent we had encountered upon the Proteus. It made it easy to believe Field's words on more than just the symbolic level, but it underlined the importance of completing our task.

"Get her done, Mr. Field."

"Aye, Mr Emery." The elder Field waved his men forward, Carlisle and Waterstone carrying the improvised battering ram between them. With one final knock upon the door, and a brief wait, the pig-iron swung back and smashed into the door. The impact landing just above the lock with enough force to splinter the thick wood and buckle the gilded metal. The door itself faltered but did not give. A second blow proved to be the charm, and with reticent steps, our group entered the empty cabin of Samuel Blethyn.

The room was of a size. Not as well furnished as told in some stories, but as broad as the ship itself and deep enough to hold a polished desk, an upholstered chair, a small cot, a chest of drawers, and two large sea-chests crafted from stained wood and brass. Upon the desk sat several charts, a sextant, a large pair of compasses, and an inkwell and pen and upon the cot lay what I presumed had been the contents of the drawers and the chests, each of which lay open and in a state of much disarray.

"Looks like someone left in a hurry." Elias Ford prodded one chest with his foot, a sullen expression which bordered on outright hatred burned deep into his features. "And no doubt with our treasure, too."

Simeon Field came to the side of the dark-haired man and peered with him into the depths of the trunk. "You think the captain has abandoned us?"

Ford huffed a great sigh, full of bitter cynicism. "A missing boat, with just enough crew to sail and defend his unearned treasure? A crew made up of men who had yet to learn of its existence, and a boat missing the minute we became becalmed, and the threat of whatever the hell these infernal waters contain was unleashed upon the Dauntless? Yes, I'd wager good money the good Captain Blethyn is no longer aboard his ship, young Field. Good money."

We, to a man, fell silent. Each of us lost in our own thoughts. Our captain was not known as the most principled man who ever sailed upon the sea, his mind ever on the profit to be earned from our expeditions. He was a slovenly man, fond of his rest and of his liquor, but I had never known him to be a cruel man. Nor a cowardly one.

"There is one alternative." William Waterstone leaned back against the wall and stroked his beard. "This may not be the captain's work at all. What if some miscreant, upon learning of this treasure you speak of, came here to claim it for himself?"

I shot Elias Ford a searching glance, which he turned away from. His attention taken by the window of the cabin and the brooding clouds which matched his demeanour so well.

"Then what of the boat, and the missing men?" He fired back over one shoulder. "How does your theorising explain that?"

"They gave up." The deep timbre of Franklin Carlisle's voice dragged with a weariness I could feel. "They realised there was no hope left upon this vessel, that remaining aboard her would only prolong their ordeal, and they escaped in the only way they thought possible."

"In one small boat? On a dead calm sea?"

Carlisle's red-rimmed eyes lifted to those of William Waterstone. "Aye." Was all he said, but that one word sparked a thousand more as each man put forward argument and counterargument, talking and shouting across and over each other in their haste to make their points. It took the hard slam of sextant on polished wood to arrest their heated words.

"Enough!" I scored the room with a hard gaze born from years of experience controlling and directing the men under my command. "I understand. I do. We all need answers. We all need someone, or something to turn to, to point to, to blame; but this is not the way." I wiped one hand across my mouth. "I suggest every man here would

171

benefit from some time alone and some rest. Therefore, as senior officer aboard, I am ordering Mr Waterstone, and Mr Carlisle below for three hours. Mr Ford, and Mr Field the elder will remain at post until then, at which point you will relieve them. Mr Field the younger, you will remain with me. Once we are all suitably refreshed and sanity can prevail, we will revisit this matter. Do I make myself clear?"

"Aye, Mr Emery," came the muttered replies.

"Then get to it!"

I watched as the last man left the cabin and turned to Simeon Field. "I am sorry to keep you from rest, Mr Field, but I need another pair of eyes, and yours are eyes I can trust. Keep them trained on Mr Ford and Mr Carlisle. If you note anything, be it of the lowest import, return and inform me. Do you understand?"

"Aye, Mr Mate." The young man snapped to attention, the movement causing his blond locks to bob back from his face. A motion filled with a confidence that never reached his eyes.

For a second time, the sounds of harsh cries awoke me. I extricated myself from the coat I had used to cover myself and rolled from the captain's cot. My senses dimmed; my mind sparked by the uproar. Once more, I ran onto the deck. The brothers Field stood to the port side, shouting and gesticulating, their arms spread wide, anger and fear writ large upon their faces. Before them stood Franklin Carlisle. The big man stripped to the waist, his muscles, drenched in sweat and blood, reflect-

172

ed the light of a torch he held in his left hand. In the right, a large curved and serrated knife gleamed. More disturbing than any of this, however, was the light that shone deep within the man's eyes as he advanced, with deliberate steps and violent intent, upon his shipmates.

"He killed them, Mr Emery." Simeon Field had spotted my approach through the murk and took two unstable steps toward me, tears streaming down his cheeks. "Billy Waterstone, Francis Cotton, Abraham Barr. They're all dead."

"They're all free," Carlisle growled. "Free of this doom we have come under. Free of the burden of endless, empty eternity. Free of this hopeless weight, crushing into us from all sides and squeezing all that is human and vital out of every ounce of our being. Leaving us cold and alone to suffer a living, conscious death." The big man began to weep. "I saved them from that hell, as I saved the men I removed from their torment and set loose upon the ship's boat. And now it seems I must save you as well."

He strode forward, still not appearing in any great rush, the knife and the torch raised before him, and I grabbed the younger Field to me, and with a shout beckoned his brother to join us. Benedict Field glanced at the two of us, back at the approaching spectre of death, and instead moved the other way, splitting the attention of the big man. He couldn't come for all of us, not at once, and even in his crazed state, the thought of two men attacking him from behind clearly didn't appeal. With a last venomous look at Benedict Field, he let loose a mighty roar and came charging towards myself and

Simeon Field. We too took the choice to spread. Field dodging to the left and myself to the right, causing Carlisle to pause once more and allowing Benedict Field the time to attack.

The elder Field had found a weapon of sorts. A heavy lantern of copper, brass and blown glass no doubt brought from below deck to aid with all-encompassing gloom. He swung this improvised flail in a mighty underhand blow at the giant's head which bent the metal, fractured the glass and sent a torrent of oil flowing onto his shoulders, along with a fresh rivulet of blood.

The impact was enough to cause the grim spectre of death we had once called shipmate to stagger heavily into the foremast. Field pressed home his advantage and dived at the man's midriff, causing a yelp of pain to escape his lips and the foremast to emit a tortured groan as the timber came under the unexpected stress. For a moment I thought Field's gallantry had been enough to allow us to win the day, but before his brother and I could hasten to his side, Carlisle let loose a mighty roar and threw his adversary to the deck, following up with unhurried but implacable steps, the knife and the torch still somehow held in his hands. I felt cold, powerless, unable to move or even to voice my horror. It was Simeon Field who acted.

The slim youth, spurred into action by his brother's plight rushed forward and dove at Franklin Carlisle, aiming not at his midriff as his brother had done but at his legs, causing the larger man to stumble and the hand holding the torch to drop to his side where it caught the lamp-oil soaking the skin of the bare-chested giant. Oil, flame, and man combining to become a mighty conflagration.

Carlisle fell to his knees, one hand raised in supplication, asking the aid of someone or something unseen by my eyes. A thick roiling smoke that carried with it a sickening smell of flesh and fire rose to join the sour fog and the salty ozone of the grim canopy which pressed down upon us. The pyre that had been Franklin Carlisle collapsed in on itself and fell to the wooden boards, fueled by much more than some small volume of lamp-oil. The flames burned red, and yellow, and green, all shot through with an incandescent white which was almost painful to look upon until, with unnatural speed and finality, they died away, leaving behind them a pile of charred bones in a circle of scorched wood.

The brothers Field pulled themselves to their feet in a movement almost synchronised and found each other's arms, their embrace a wordless testament to the depths of their fraternal love. I gazed on; a strange and poignant jealousy surfacing within me for a moment, only to be swallowed once more by a heartfelt gratitude for the safety of my men. It was then, with the heat of battle behind us, I noted for the first time how the younger field was dressed.

The short trousers and white hose were the same as I'd seen him wear so many times before, as was the white linen shirt. What I now noted, what I should have noted before, was that upon this day, Simeon Field had paired these with a blue jacket and a red woolen cap. Dressed in this fashion, the tall, blonde-haired youth roused a memory that caused my heart to pause in its rhythm and the moisture to leech from my mouth, as fear, cold and insidious, grabbed hold of me and promised never to let me go.

"Mr Field." My cry caused both men to turn toward me. "Simeon. Your cap. Where did it come from?"

Their expressions turned to incredulous wonderment.

"My cap? Why, I found it. Below deck, as I followed Elias Ford. I assumed it to be his."

"You followed Ford? Why?" Consternation still haunted Benedict Field's eyes.

"Mr Emery told me to, and he was right to do so, too." He turned his attention back my way. "You were right, Mr Emery. Ford was up to something. He had this silver box with him, all polished metal and filigree."

"The treasure." The elder Field pulled away from his brother and limped toward me. "That selfish, greedy cur has our salvaged treasure, but that means…"

"It means he killed Samuel Blethyn." I finished Field's sentence for him. "And maybe more, too."

"Waterstone? Barr? You think Ford guilty of those crimes?"

"I don't know. This storm, this ship. It's doing something to us. All of us. There is something acting to pervert us. To turn us against each other and against ourselves, too. It is as if we have become actors in some play, as if…"

I think it was then I finally knew what devilment the cursed ship Proteus had in store for us. The enormity of it all but unthinkable, and deep within something grabbed ahold of me, choking the words back, forcing me into silence.

"He took it to the hold." Simeon Field supplied the words I knew must come. "He had food with him, too. And he had armed himself with a pistol and a gully knife."

"Then he plans to batten down the hatches and wait out the voyage." Benedict focused on his brother; my presence forgotten. "Either that or creep back up on deck while we rest and butcher us one by one."

The younger Field's eyes narrowed and for a moment his youthful features hardened. "That's what I'd do."

"Then let us ensure he never gets the chance. Come, Simeon, and bring your knife. Mr Emery, do you stand with us?"

I wanted to say no. I wanted to stop them. To tell them they headed to their doom. But something would not allow the words to be voiced. The infernal pressure of the brooding sky closed in around me, pressing down, crushing me, filling me with its acrid vapours until the air to speak was robbed from me. A fresh layer of mist rose from the too-still waters below and I fancied I heard a voice hidden in its depths. A voice urging me to obey. To submit. Despair gripped me. Any hope I might have once held dashed against some rocky shoreline within. I was nothing. Nobody. And all I could do was submit. Without will or conscious thought, I trailed in the wake of Simeon Field as we both followed his brother into the bowels of the ship.

***

The scene in the galley was one of gore and death. Two bodies lay strewn on the floor. One beneath the suspended table, and one against the galley's range. The fresh, sticky evidence of the manner of their deaths pooled and splattered all about this charnel house, and creeping up to meet it from beneath the boards and the bottom of each wall was a black and noisome tar. A foul mass which would, no doubt, climb steadily toward the deck above.

Benedict and Simeon Field ran through this destruction as if it were not there and bolted down the steps to the hold below, needing neither lantern nor flame to see. I followed behind a faithful, obedient slave to an unknown master.

If what follows lacks colour or detail, then I can only apologise, for it was in some half-woken state I watched as Benedict Field reached the bottom step and discovered the crazed and feral man who I had once known as Elias Field. He hunkered amongst bolts of cloth, now dyed an indelible black, with his teeth bared and a billhook in his hand. It was with morbid detachment I saw the blade bite into Benedict's neck and spill his life's blood and how Simeon Field, taking a lesson from his encounter with Franklin Carlisle, launched at his legs, stopping his second blow, and taking him to the ground to kneel upon his chest; fists flying into his face.

I might have helped. Might have come rushing to my crewmate's aid, but it was as if everything human and feeling, every ounce of compassion and mercy, had left me. Instead, I merely watched on, as if from inside some immobile statue, as Ford thrust up his billhook and pierced the younger Field through the side as he raised his hand for another punch. The blonde lad cried out, a mighty bellow of pain and grief, and wrapped his hands around his killer's neck, wringing the life out of him. Only when Ford's eyes bulged for the last time and he lay still amongst the decaying cargo and thick, unctuous rot, his tongue protruding from his open mouth did Simeon Field, the boy who would follow in his brother's footsteps, fall bodily against a rotting bolt of cotton and die.

This is a warning. I believe I have made that much clear. It is a warning to leave this ship. Leave it now and never once think of returning. As I write, the noisome, tar-like substance has taken over this ship, infecting all before it with decay, and although the storm clouds have lifted, the ship remains trapped in its own perpetual gloom. The Proteus is sunk. I saw myself its inelegant demise as the waves lapped over the shattered timbers of a once proud ship for the last time. Yes, the Proteus is sunk, but it is not gone. It lives on. Here. In the boards and the rigging of a ship which was once named Dauntless, now a rotting hulk, infested with an unholy canker that has risen from its depths to lie upon every part of the vessel, its foremast leaning, a section of boards near the Fo'c's'le blasted by flame.

It exists in the souls of all the men who died aboard, their remains absorbed by the vessel, or left as a trap for the unwary. It dwells in the greed of Elias Ford and the empty and the murderous despair of Franklin Carlisle; in the desperate protective love of one brother to another and in the spectral figure of Simeon Field, the innocent youth now doomed to walk this ship forever more, an undead guide to eternal damnation.

And, of course, the Proteus lives on in me, too.

We never disturbed the captain's quarters of the Proteus, we never thought to. I think somehow the ship kept us from the idea, but I cannot shake the thought that on the desk, by the side of the inkwell, lay a document like this. A tale written to warn us of the fate we were about to put upon ourselves. It is a tantalising idea, one which seems somehow right, but it is one which I can never confirm. All I can do is write my warning and pray it is enough.

As for me, my fate is sealed. It was from the moment I saw a stricken ship and thought to save an injured sailor. Now I am to serve upon this new Proteus forever, not as its Mate, nor as its captain, but as a physical rendition of the warning I wish to deliver.

The voice of the vessel calls me, even now, and soon I must obey. I will go to the prow of the ship and take firm hold of my double ended trident. And there I will stand for all eternity, even as the ship reconfigures around me, integrating my form into its design. My limbs will stiffen, my legs fuse and elongate, my skin harden and numb, until the merchant brig, Proteus, has a figurehead once more.

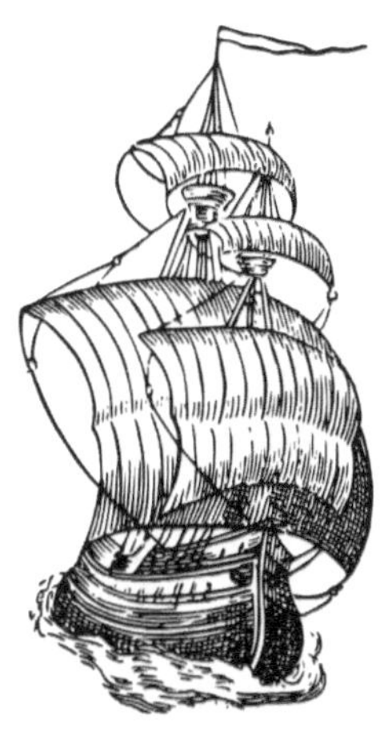

THE FATHOMLESS

S.O. GREEN

There was freedom on the waves.

Hard to chart your own course when you were confined by cobbles and cruelty, where the nights were broken by ragged coughing and the mornings tainted by mother's wails as another of your siblings failed to wake. Where the mist hid knives and the cost of a life could be gauged by the price of a bracelet in a pawn shop. Where life hung by a thread from a spinning mule and the price for incaution was an arm.

That was the London Jack knew, and it was the London he had fled. Better to sail, his father had said, being a Navy man himself, though the Navy wouldn't have Jack. So a black flag it would have to be.

From a stowaway to a captain in ten years, he'd proven himself worthy of the jacket and the tricorn and the spyglass he carried in his pocket. Proven it with blood—his own and others—spilled by cutlass and club and roaring flintlock. He'd protected his home, supported his family, dealt justice where it was needed. When the captain's old wound had finally caught up to him and they'd found him in his cabin, rotten through, no one had disputed Jack's right to fill the space he'd left behind.

It was already his, anyway.

He'd become a man aboard that ship, worked the weakness out of his body one agonising day at a time. The ropes had turned his hands to leather and broadened his shoulders to fit the beloved jacket. The scar on his lip, on his eyebrow, reminded the others what happened to those who tried to take what was his. And it reminded them what would happen if anyone tried to harm them, because Jack stood for his crew, his family.

A man in all particulars but one.

He had been the one to spy the Alexandria off their port side, listing like a drunken man without a wall to lean against. A brigantine, hopefully with a small crew and a large hold. It was flying British colours and Jack, ever a patriot, decided it was their duty to check on the vessel's crew.

"They might have cargo in need of rescuing," he'd said, and the others had laughed and retrieved their cudgels.

When they drew abreast, half the crew—Jack included—swung across to the Alexandria's deck from their schooner. The sea churned beneath his boots, salt spit whipping between the boards and lashing his cheeks.

To die on the sea, and be swallowed into that blue oblivion, felt so much more fitting than a pine box and six feet of cold dirt. The fish would take his flesh; his bones would join the coral on the ocean floor. There was no end more perfect.

Jack touched down and skidded on something slathered across the deck. The other men did the same, fighting for balance. Crimson, thick and brine-speck-led, gathering in lakes between the corpses all around. It dribbled out through the scuppers like the ship was crying red tears.

The stench put Jack in mind of the slaughterhouse his family had lived behind, and the rivers of offal that had flowed past their tin shack daily. Bubbling, heaving masses of what had once been living things, but which lived no longer. It reminded him of the day Tim had dragged home half a pig as large as he was. Pork for dinner.

And the way Tim had danced when they'd hung him for it. They'd brought a barrel for him to stand on because his ten-year-old neck couldn't reach the noose.

"What in God's name...?" the mate gasped.

"Blasphemy, Terrence," Jack warned with a smirk.

His first mate mopped his brow with a mono-grammed handkerchief that didn't bear his initials. Stocky and rotund, he wore an old naval jacket that was obliged to remain unbuttoned, though there was some debate about whether he'd ever served that particular navy. His white whiskers made him the grandfather Jack had never had, just as the Captain had been the father. The red on his cheeks betrayed a love of drink that seemed to run in the family.

Five chests were gathered on the deck, all locked. They had slid against the starboard bulwark and tilted the vessel in the water. And, with the crew in bloody repose, there was no one to correct the imbalance. Jack's crew would oblige, and they'd be paid well for the privilege.

"Steer us upright," he ordered, "and let's see what they've got for us."

Half the crew dragged the chests back to centre. Each one was heavy with the promise of riches, except one which was surprisingly light by comparison. The slant in the deck evened out. It was just a little easier walking in all that blood now.

"What happened, do you think?" Terrence asked, as the others heaved the bodies aside and laid them out like it was a wake.

There were over a dozen of them—shot, stabbed, beaten. It reminded Jack of something.

"Fifteen men on a dead man's chest," he muttered.

"Beg pardon, Captain?"

"Nothing. I'd guess this was a result of the greed that is natural to men of the sea." Jack shrugged. "Honestly, it just saves us a job, doesn't it?"

"Should we blow them open?" one of the others suggested, patting one of the strong boxes.

"You're far too eager to waste gunpowder. Shall we have a look for the keys first? If anyone finds them, I'll be in the captain's quarters."

They busied themselves with the search, and Jack

pushed open the door to the cabin at the vessel's stern. It had been a good day thus far. Not a single drop of blood spilled—from his men, at any rate—and the promise of five full chests.

Well... Four and a half.

He found the captain of the Alexandria sitting at his table. Someone had stitched four bright red buttons on his chest. They'd dyed his blouson* and pantaloons and filled up his boots too, by the looks of things. Jack doffed his hat, then set about looting the place.

The man didn't have as fine a jacket or hat as Jack, which was always a mark of some pride. His spyglass was nicer though—polished brass and crystal, the very best—so he half-inched it. It wasn't like the poor captain would be needing it.

There was a bottle at his still right hand and an empty tumbler.

"Yo-ho-ho, and a bottle of rum," Jack said, and poured himself a drink. "Cheers, sir. It's only right I salute you. Your misfortune's good business for me and mine."

A search of the cabin revealed what Jack first mistook for vanity. The jewellery, the perfume, the full-length mirror fixed to the floor of the cabin—wasn't the old captain a strutting peacock?

Then Jack found the dress and realised that perhaps the truth was more complicated than that. It was a soft thing, green satin and trimmed with lace, meant for a curvy, slender type. Jack stood at the mirror and held the dress against his front, head cocked, wondering.

No. It would look terrible, and the skin under his

binder itched just thinking about it.

But it would sell when they got back to port. The jewellery in its box; the ornate comb; the scented water in its pretty glass bottle. They'd all fetch a tidy sum. He'd get the crew good and drunk and they'd raise him on their shoulders and carry him back to the ship, singing, chanting his name, and he'd remember, for another day, who he really was.

He'd come back for it all later. The captain's jacket held the keys, an iron bunch in the inner pocket that jangled as Jack lifted them free. One of them was stained red where the bullet holes had bled through the material. Jack swung them around his finger and strode out onto the deck, heels clicking.

"Looking for these, gentlemen?" he asked, and tossed the ring to Terrence.

His mate grinned and set about the gratifying task of unlocking five iron-edged chests. The trinkets from the captain's cabin alone would have made this little excursion worthwhile, but this?

This had the potential to be something very special.

The first chest didn't disappoint. The sunlight caught the gold inside and dazzled, as gold so often did. The crew descended with giddy laughter, scooping up coins and letting them fall, counting bottles and pipes and plump women with every one that clinked into the pile. They spread their delight over the second and third chests as Terrence worked.

"This reminds me of the chests we carried into the Portuguese territories," the mate said. "Filled with gold and jewels, they were. Never saw the like before or since."

Jack laughed. "Another story from your days as an honest sailor?"

It was one of the reasons Terrence made such an excellent second. Not just his experience, or his time as a naval officer, but the fact he was honourable, in his way. It meant Jack didn't have to worry about waking up with a knife in his chest, or worse.

Between the two of them, they steered a (relatively) straight course.

"They were a tribute for the tribal chiefs. A good-will gesture."

"Well, the tribute's ours now. Every last coin of it."

Terrence flicked Jack a gap-toothed smile and turned to the last chest. He took the blood-stained key and turned it in the lock. The moment the lid was raised, he recoiled with another blasphemy. Stronger this time.

Jack stepped forward and peered into the chest. The men who weren't occupied with admiring their new-found wealth joined him.

And they saw the woman lying in the bottom of the box—shift filthy, fingernails bloody—and the scratches in the underside of the lid.

Jack was the first to approach. He reached through the matted nest of what might have been blonde hair and felt around the wretch's neck. There, thready and weak, a pulse.

"She's still alive. Get her back to the ship."

"It's bad luck, taking a woman on board," Terrence grunted.

"With respect, Terrence, that's shite and you know

it. Put her in my cabin. And if bad luck comes for us, send it straight to me."

They set a fire aboard the Alexandria to speed it to its grave, and because the crew loved a good fire. Jack watched it from the window of his cabin, growing brighter as the flames caught and the night began to deepen around them. By the time the sun sank beneath the azure horizon, the conflagration on the waters still held his eye, but it was enough away now they couldn't be implicated.

Four chests full of gold, jewels, and assorted treasures. The perfect haul. Soured only slightly by the unpleasant surprise in the fifth.

She was beautiful, Jack had decided. Once they lay her out on his bed and Jack had smoothed the hair away from her face, he could see the fullness of her lips and the thickness of her lashes, a prettiness in the angles of her features that begged for a smile.

She had a figure that demanded more than that dirty shift, too. Jack's mind went to the dress. It had been meant for her, that much was clear. He pulled it from the sack he'd stuffed it in, along with all the other trinkets he'd found in the captain's cabin and hung it from a peg near the bed. Perhaps, when she awoke, she'd prefer a change of clothes.

She wouldn't cause trouble; Jack was sure of that. They'd drop her in the nearest port and sail away, and that would be the end of it. He told himself that as he locked his cabin door and tucked a loaded flintlock into his belt.

No, the woman wouldn't cause trouble. And if the men tried, they wouldn't find Jack in a mood to entertain.

He sat by the bedside, with the captain's rum providing company while he waited on the girl.

Drink and the devil had done for the rest...

In the light from the lantern, she looked angelic. And, with the shifting of the shadows, he noticed something he hadn't noticed before.

It was a cord, around her neck. He reached for it, lifted it from the front of her shift. The knot came loose, and he lifted the pendant into the light, where he could see it properly.

It looked like a seashell, with a mark inscribed on it that he didn't recognise. A mark that pulsed and swelled with the waves beating against the boards below. His eyes started to ache the longer he looked at it, until eventually he had to put it down.

He blinked, trying to rid himself of the pain and the sudden feeling of seasickness.

Jack hadn't been seasick in over ten years.

"That symbol belongs to the King in Blue."

Jack started. The woman was staring at him. She hadn't moved from the bed, hadn't tried to sit up, but her eyes were open and focused. Jack felt heat climbing in his cheeks.

"Who's that?"

"You don't know about the King in Blue? The Deep One? The Fathomless?"

"Giving me more riddles won't help me solve the first one."

"I'm sorry. I assumed you were part of a new crew sent to relieve the last one, but..."

She pushed herself up on the bed. Unconscious, she'd been like a doll, pale and fragile. Awake, she had dignity and poise, and Jack had the sudden urge to take off his hat. Her stare lanced through him and he got the distinct impression he was beneath her. Captain or not.

"Do you serve the king?"

"In Blue, or Of England?"

"The latter, but I can tell by the undignified way you speak that you do not. You aren't from a relief crew, are you? You're some kind of pirate."

"You're not quite as clueless as I'd expected for a woman that was locked in a box."

The weight of her gaze was the pressure at the bottom of the sea. Her eyes glistened, aquamarine, and Jack's questions about her took on new depths.

"I was to be part of the tribute. That was my duty. When we set sail, all the roles were clear. The captain entertained me in his cabin by night and, by day, I made my peace with the world above the surface, knowing I would never see it again. But, over time, I think the captain developed a fondness for me. He decided that I would belong to him, rather than the King in Blue."

"And how did you feel about that?"

"Angry. I had only just resigned myself to my fate. Now, another man had decided to make me property and undo what had been done. When I would not come quietly, he..."

"Locked you in a chest like a piece of treasure."

The woman's withering look couldn't cover up the

fact that Jack was absolutely correct.

"Half of the crew sided with him, because he offered to pay them with riches that weren't his to give."

"The other chests."

"But the other half of the crew understood the importance of what we were trying to do. They stood against him."

"They wiped each other out. Not a single man was left alive when we boarded."

And they lay there that had took the plumb, with sightless glare and their lips struck dumb...

"Then I suppose you are more innocent than I first thought, assuming that I believe a word you are saying."

Jack laughed. No one had used the word innocent to describe him in a good, long time.

"So, now that we've cleared up what happened aboard your ship, are you going to tell me who this King in Blue is, and why you were going to be offered in tribute to him?"

"If I have to explain it then you'll never understand."

"You take far too much pleasure in being an enigma."

"I don't take any pleasure in it. Trust me." She considered for a moment and then nodded, sure of what she had decided. "The responsibility rests with you now. Deliver the tribute."

"I'm not really one for responsibility."

"You must do it. For the Empire. These seas do not belong to us and, without the promised offering, they will be taken from us all. Have you not benefited from the Empire and the ocean both?"

Jack scoffed. "Have I benefited from the Empire? Shall I tell you a story? My mum was a seamstress. She made pretty clothes for the high-born ladies just like you. When I was twelve years old, they took her to the courthouse, and she never came home. Transportation, the neighbours told me. She probably died before she ever arrived. Do you know what she was accused of?" Jack pointed at the dress, dangling from its peg like a ten-year-old boy who'd stolen a side of pork. "Theft. Because she chose not to deliver a dress she hadn't been paid for. Your Empire and your ocean took what they wanted from me. Am I not allowed to take back?"

"We all have our role to play. One way or another."

Jack sighed and rose from his seat. He took the bottle but left the rest.

"I'll lock the door on my way out. You'll be safe here. I'm dropping you at the nearest port but the gold is mine now. Whatever you want to do after that is none of my business."

He'd walked to the door before the woman spoke again.

She said, "Understand that, no matter what happens, I bear you no ill will."

Jack scoffed and stepped out onto the deck. He needed some time to clear his head. Speaking with the woman was like riding the edge of a whirlpool, and it left him spinning.

He took the slap of the briny air on his cheeks and went in search of Terrence.

He found his mate standing at the bulwark on the port side, staring out across the moonlit waves. The night was still, and the sky was clear. The doldrums had swallowed them up all of a sudden. Jack would pray for wind on the morrow.

"Any bad luck found us yet?" he asked, slapping the other man on the shoulder and offering him the bottle.

Terrence declined. Now Jack was *really* worried. "Give it time, Captain. There's no outrunning it if it's meant to find you."

"You worry too much."

"I wouldn't have to if you worried just a little more."

"I'd rather leave it to you. I mean, you're so good at it."

Jack flashed him a grin. It was enough to get the old sailor chuckling. They'd made a good team, even before Jack donned the tricorn, and the men seemed to appreciate their combined leadership.

Jack gave them direction, impetus, and Terrence gave them stability.

"She'll be trouble," the mate grumbled, breath fogging in the chill air.

"Not every woman is a harbinger of pain and misery, Terrence. You're too old-fashioned."

"I'm not talking about that, boy. I don't actually believe they bring bad luck aboard. Mostly, it's just to get the men to leave well enough alone. Do you know what happens to women aboard a vessel like this, out on the sea for months at a time, crewed only by lonely, desperate sailors?"

"The same thing that happens to them on foggy London streets, I reckon. It's nothing to do with the ship, Terrence. It's to do with the men. And ours are good men."

"What makes you think she's a good woman? The fact that she was locked in a box? Or the fact that she has the face of an angel? Don't think I didn't see you fawning over her."

"I wasn't fawning," Jack grunted, and hesitated because his mother had told him never to lie, "that much."

"She sparked a covetous look in your eye, boy. And it's made you paranoid, unless you thought I hadn't noticed the pistol you're carrying. See, even good men can get twisted up, but make no mistake. You wouldn't be the first captain who'd been foolish enough to fall for her. I don't much fancy being the next crew to burn."

"You're my crew, Terrence. And I'm not going to let you burn."

They gazed skyward and Jack's eyes slipped between the twinkling stars, the map to guide them home, to the void beyond that promised nothing but emptiness.

All lookouts clapped on paradise; all souls bound just contrariwise...

"What's going on?"

Jack looked around. Terrence backed away from the rail, shaking his head. The deck tilted like the Alexandria's. Except that the chests were secured below, and the weight distributed evenly, which meant that something was dragging them to one side. And it wasn't the non-existent wind.

"Wake the men," Jack ordered. "We need to fix this."

Terrence nodded and hurried below decks. Jack drew the flintlock from his belt and marched back to his cabin.

Trouble had come to his ship, and it wasn't welcome.

He found the woman still sitting on his bunk, arms curled around her knees. Her dignity had shrivelled and now she looked small, vulnerable. No longer the lucky survivor of a massacre, because what came after might well have been worse than the death and the blood.

"What's happening to my ship?" Jack demanded. "And don't tell me any riddles. I'm not drunk enough to be amused."

"It's the King. He's here for his tribute."

"How? There weren't any other ships out there? It's quiet as the grave out there. We'd have seen him coming a mile off and put a hole through whatever fancy rigging he was flying."

"You don't understand," she said, lifting her head enough that Jack could see the tears shining on her cheeks. "You don't understand anything."

He didn't like to admit that she was right, because he understood plenty of things. He'd understood how much his life was worth in old London town, and he'd understood how much his value would climb aboard a ship if he could prove himself. He understood how to use the winds, how to navigate by the stars, how to stir the hearts of his crew. That wasn't worth nothing.

Except that she was right. Jack didn't understand any of this.

There was a cry from below decks, the boom of a blunderbuss firing, the sound of tortured wood tearing, splitting apart. The ship shook, and the listing worsened. Jack leaned into the tilt and growled.

"Stay here," he ordered, and stormed out.

He made to follow Terrence's trail down to quarters and the hold where they'd secured the chests, taking a pull from the bottle on his way. For courage. He recoiled when he saw the water rising from below, frothing white and hungering for his ship.

Of Terrence and the others, there was no sign.

"What the bloody hell is going on?"

The answer to Jack's question rose from the churning water and stepped onto the deck, waterlogged feet squelching on the planks. It might loosely have been described as a man, if a man had translucent skin threaded with blue veins and profusions of wriggling tendrils where its fingers and toes should have been and eyes that looked to be inside out glaring hard from features deformed by quivering, slithering strands of flesh, moving like an octopus dancing through the ocean.

And if a man would wear a coral crown perched atop his head.

"My tribute," it gurgled, and held out one gelatinous hand.

"You've already taken all the bloody treasure!" Jack snarled. "And everything else, too. My crew, my ship. What more do you want?"

196

"One was chosen to be my tribute. I only desire what was promised to me. Decide. Now."

Decide what? The answer came a second after the question. There were only two of them left alive. Jack and the woman. So which of them would it be?

Soft, slender hands curled around Jack's throat. He didn't understand what was happening until he felt the cord knotting at the back of his neck, before he felt the weight of the inscribed shell resting against his chest.

Until he heard the woman's voice whispering, "I'm sorry."

The King reached for him. He lifted the flintlock and pulled the trigger. A clump of tentacles clubbed his arm aside, and the ball exploded into the sky with a crack and a blast of smoke. Then the slithering fingers curled around his wrist and broke bones with a crack-crack-snap. The pistol tumbled from his useless hand and bounced off the deck.

Jack wrestled free and turned to run, though where could anyone run on the ocean? Something wrapped around his ankle and jerked him off his feet. His chin struck the deck and red burst from his mouth. His tricorn tumbled off, chestnut hair spilling in ribbons down his shoulders, soaking brine from the lashing waves. His binder tore under his shirt, and a scream ripped from his throat as the thing started to drag him away. His fingernails splintered on the boards. Prayers burst like bubbles on his bloody lips.

The woman watched, still weeping but face expressionless, and Jack wondered how he'd ever believed there was freedom on the waves. How could a woman

ever be free to chart her own course when kings demanded tribute to be paid in gold and flesh? When they were
possessions to be traded, taken and given? When their
only choice was to go or send another in their place?

The King dragged him to the rail, and he stared
down into the rising tide. Perhaps the woman would find
the blue oblivion he had yearned for, but the thing had a
different fate picked out for Jack.

It carried him over the bulwark, and the scream
hadn't left his lips before they broke the surface and the
water rushed in.

Ten fathoms deep on the road to Hell...

The ocean stole his scream and poured in to fill the
space that air had once taken up. Fate being merciless, he
didn't die, and wouldn't for an eternity to come.

And, when the bubbles burst and the surface stilled,
one last piece of Jack the pirate, Jack the man, bobbed
back up.

Yo-ho-ho, and a bottle of rum...

WHAT LIES ON THE OTHER SIDE

STEPHEN JOHNSON

The cold dark splash boomed across the side of the worn battle tested wood on the bow, lunging the once mighty ship starboard as the helmsman fought to maintain course.

"Captain, the winds are pushing us hard starboard. I can't keep her steady." The young deck hand shouted over the blistering sideways rain and howling wind. As he spoke, a large powerful wave crashed into the port side beak head, nearly ripping the ornately carved mermaid affectionately called Dorothy off the deck.

"Boatswain, shorten the main sail, now!" The grizzled man behind the young helmsman named Mira roared out.

The burly Boatswain's Mate rang out deeply, "Aye, aye, Captain," before scampering off and barking orders at the few hands on deck.

"Mr Johnson, I want to be off the coast of St. Kitts by morning, you understand? I will not lose that British Galleon again! Are we clear?"

I brushed the water from my old spectacles and gave the most confident, "Aye, aye," I could muster under the conditions and went back to managing the deck hands with the sails. Don't screw this up, I whispered to myself. It had been at least two weeks since the last time we came across the Expedition, the jewel of the English fleet. A 40-gun behemoth English War Galleon that patrolled the Caribbean unmercifully, its sole mission was the eradication of our way of life—the pirate way of life.

As we travelled the last three months aboard the Ferocity, or Fero as we liked to call her, the Captain's singular focus remained on the dreaded hunter ship, Expedition, not for revenge mind you. No, we sought something much more rewarding and self-satisfying than revenge. Gold. As the right hand of the Captain, the ship's First Mate, I was privy to all of his thoughts as well. He knew what others did not about the fabled English galleon. While she was very successful in eliminating pirate ships and crews, she took on what she wanted in plunder before sending them to meet Davy Jones. As the Captain liked to exclaim, "Now you tell me who the true pirate is, my lad."

After a few hours of deadly winds and rain, the weather topside rescinded, and the waters calmed, spilling out into a beautiful and tranquil horizon. The sun began to peak through the clouds and heat the warm Caribbean waters as we hoisted all sails for full sailing and rigged the ship for our best speed. I travelled down below, exhausted, to my small cabin I shared with the Gunner's Mate. A master of all weapon types, I rarely saw him as he spent the majority of his time tending to our battery of guns along the sides of the mighty Ferocity. I entered my cabin and immediately fell into the rack. Sleep arrived instantly as I closed my eyes and let the early morning hours drift away.

I felt a hand shaking me as I jumped from my slumber. The young helmsman, Mira, nervously stood over me.

"Mr Johnson, come quick, Sir. There is something on the main deck you have to see. I don't..." his voice trailed off in a stutter.

I cleared the sleep from my eyes and looked at the young man's face to see him clearly spooked and terrified. "Very well," I muttered as I jumped from my rack and started to follow him topside. I kept a small mirror in the side of my cabin. Although dingy and worn, it served its purpose on occasion. I glanced back again as something in the reflection caught my eye. Strange, I thought.

I was moving so quickly I had to stop and even took a step backward to look at the mirror again, but this time all I saw was my familiar weathered face staring back. I shook my head and cursed for delaying and immediately sprinted up after the young man. Still, my mind drifted back to the image I saw in the mirror my initial glance caught before leaving. The reflection was my face but it seemed to be sneering back towards me with the most sinister look, but it was not there when I turned back to look the second time. Again, I shook my head and let sensible rationalisation take over. You have slept for four hours over the last two days and are just tired, just let it go.

Walking out onto the deck, the weather was so different from when I had left. The ferocious storm was now replaced by calm peaceful still waters. The sun though was overcast, and the sky was almost dark. The peace upon the sea brought more of a chill to my spine than comfort. I followed the young deck hand to the bow and joined the Boatswain's Mate as he peered over the side of the ship.

"So, Boats, what is this unexplainable thing you seem to have found and have you briefed the Captain yet?"

I spoke rapidly to the man with a slight bit of irritation from being awoken after only a few hours of sleep but stopped speechless as I looked down into the water under the dark sky. The air had turned briskly cold and I felt a shiver crawl down my spine as I stared into the vast abyss below me. The calm blue water stretched out all around us except for the small patch off to the starboard side of the bow and I could now see why the man was so confused and afraid. The water glowed with a green fluorescence that seemed to sheen off the top of the water. The air was freezing and a strange putrid smell filled the air.

Boats looked blankly back at me and started to speak, "No sir, we have not briefed the Captain," his voice trailed off as he searched for words.

I nodded nervously and leaned over to get a closer look. The young helmsman and Boats stood behind me. "Lookouts have scanned the rest of the horizon but this is the only place showing this kind of," he paused for a second, "anomaly, I suppose is the best word for it."

I stared back at Boats as he returned his gaze back towards the water. He continued, "We put a small boat in the water to measure it. Lad said the water was freezing and that strange green glow went on all the way to the bottom of the ocean, Sir. He reckoned it measured about 1000 yards by 3000 yards total, almost perfectly shaped like a large door." He let the last word linger for a moment as he put a special emphasis on it.

"About the only other thing we can measure is the temperature. Dropped a line into that green stuff and the line came back frozen after only a few feet." He shuddered as he finished his briefing. My concentration was suddenly interrupted as the emergency bell rang loudly from the forecastle as the messenger of the watch ran about alerting the crew to a fire below decks.

I arrived at the incident just as the fire was being put out. The crew was well trained and I was not surprised to find them performing their duties. Even aboard a rogue pirate ship, we take our damage control seriously. The Ferocity was our home and every man onboard treated her as such.

Everyone looked in order except my attention was drawn over to the corner of the space where one of the younger lads was standing. I did not recognise the young man but knew he had recently come aboard in St. Martin eager to live a life on the high seas full of adventure and treasure seeking. Little did he realise the menial tasks that go into even the adventurous life of a young pirate aboard a ship at sea.

I was not so much worried about why he was standing by himself, but only because of the way he was standing there—just staring out into space with a weird and demented smile. His lower lip looked to be deformed with traces of blood spotting his chin. I started to approach the young man when I noticed a small fire still burning in the corner. I directed it to be put out and when I turned around to look for the young man, he was gone.

I tried to shake off the last few moments of stress and clear my head as I grabbed a bottle of rum in the galley. I sat down to relax for a few minutes before I planned to talk with the Captain when I noticed two men walk in. Both men walked in silently and did not acknowledge me. Strange, as it is custom for us to recognise a chain of command. Even in our pirate culture, we hold the Captain and his First Mate in high esteem, or more accurately, in awe because of fear. We have the power to make a pirate's life very profitable, or shall we say very unreasonable. I stood up and walked toward them to reprimand them when they both turned, and I noticed the same smiling sneer the young man from earlier carried. I felt the hair stand up on my arms.

"What are you doing?" I stuttered as my voice cracked and embarrassment blushed across my face. Both men just continued to stare back at me with that devilish grin, and then turned and left without muttering a word.

I watched speechless as the two men exited the room, as silent as they had entered.

I downed the rum and quickly followed them out, intent on finishing the conversation. As I exited the galley, I passed by the regular crew's berthing and noticed a young man sitting solemnly on his rack, staring into space, a bewildered look on his face. Upon closer inspection, it was the strange young man from the fire earlier. I called out to him, but he just sat silently. I entered the room and called out to him again, more sternly. The man did not respond and never moved to acknowledge me. Frustrated now after a second disrespectful episode, I walked over to face the man, "What the hell is going..."

My voice abruptly stopped and cut off as I stood in front of the young man and saw him scratching at his eyes.

The man was not only scratching his eyes, but I noticed blood-soaked cheeks and the absence of his left eye. The young man scratched desperately at the remaining eye trying to gouge it out with his fingernails—all with a sly smile on his face. I backed up slowly and almost tripped over leaving the space.

"Why, what are you doing?" I screamed out.

The door opened on the other side of the space and the two men from the galley entered, but this time they did not ignore me, locking their eyes on mine. I stopped and started to yell at them to stand down but stood in shock as I watched both men open their mouths to speak, but only a shrill scream emanated from both. The pitch caused me to fall to my knees as the sound pierced my ears. I covered my head with my hands to try and block out the noise. Blood droplets formed on my palms as my eardrums felt like they would burst.

I bolted up as the pain in my head reached unbearable levels and ran towards the door, barrelling past the two men and escaping their grip as I ran down the corridor and made my way toward the Captain's cabin. I turned back to see if I was being followed and noticed no one behind me. As I continued up the ladder, I heard a loud banging against the side of the ship and lost my balance as the ship keeled to the starboard side drastically. I heard shouts coming through the portholes from above, men screaming and in panic. Another sudden jolt and I fell to the deck, banging my head against the side of a wooden table. I felt the world go dark around me as a tremendous pain rocked through my head from the fall.

***

I woke up and felt the large lump on the back of my head. Looking around, the space seemed abandoned and quiet. I stood up slowly and strangely felt the ship rocking violently to the port and starboard. I used the table in front of me to brace as I sat awkwardly in a chair to regain my balance. I found a small mirror on the table and picked it up to see if I could see the damage to the back of my head when I saw the figure from my cabin again. I shuddered as I watched the reflection eerily smiling back at me. I dropped the mirror and it broke on the deck below me as I stood with my hands shaking. I jumped from the seat and tried to move to the main sail deck, but the swaying made traversing difficult as I moved up one ladder to the next.

As I climbed to reach the main deck, I stopped and

saw several of the crew standing motionless in a semi circle surrounding a small wooden rope locker. I approached slowly and quietly to see what the group was staring at and froze when I noticed a small mirror sitting in the middle of the group. The entire group looked toward the centre of the mirror in unison, each with a sinister smile and sneer but now with eyes black as coal. I stared behind the group and watched one of the young men walk up to the mirror and stare straight down into the reflection. I watched as a dark wrinkled hand extended out of the mirror, appearing to be coming out vertically from the flat wooden top. The hand grasped the young man's forehead and pulled him close to the mirror until his head disappeared into the reflection.

I gasped and backed away, bumping into the main mast and banging my head. I reached up to rub the pain from the collision and looked back up to see the young man's head reappearing from the mirror reflection, only now with a different look. The hand from the mirror retreated back into its home, but the young man stood staring back at me with the same black cold eyes and the devilish grin. Shuttering, I scrambled back on my hands and knees looking on as the young man who looked all of eighteen years old seemed to age fifty years before me.

"Come join us, Mr Johnson, everyone is welcome on the other side," the young man muttered in a hoarse and painful low voice and then erupted into a hysterical, deafening laugh.

The laugh alerted the rest of the group to my presence and they all turned to meet the young man's gaze. A man walked out in front of the group and the sight froze me in place.

"Captain, no, not you too!"

The Captain's head tilted back, exposing his throat and a large slit across the neck. The slit opened revealed a large eye that began blinking rapidly. I stumbled back as the group began to walk towards me on the deck. While the eye blinked its cold stare across the room, the Captain's voice spewed up directed at the ceiling, "There is nowhere to run, Mr Johnson. We see everything."

The rest of the group joined the Captain's crazed laughter and I turned to run toward the ladder well behind me looking for any escape. I quickly descended, desperate to escape the mutinous crew above, hoping to run across anyone still normal or at least not exposed to the effects of those mirrors. It seemed crazy, but from what I could ascertain, the mirror seemed to pull you through to some other place but on returning, it changed its victim. That was evident from the Captain and the rest of the crew I had just encountered.

I moved rapidly toward the Armoury, trying to formulate some sort of plan. In the meantime though, I placed my trust in a pistol and sword, my best options for survival. I heard a dull banging from a small, closed door to my right side, followed by a soft whisper from behind the door. "Is anyone out there?"

I reached for the door but thought against it, remembering the young man from earlier who scratched out his eyes. "This is Mr Johnson. Who is in there," I spoke through the door, hoping desperately for another person not infected with whatever this mirror was doing.

"It is Boats and Deck Hand Mira, Sir," a voice from behind the door said quietly. "The door is secured from the outside and we are locked in here. Some crazy stuff going on out there."

I looked around. "Are there any mirrors in there?" I waited for a reply.

"What? Mirrors? What does that matter, Sir?" The Boatswain's Mate offered up from inside the space.

I spoke in a stern voice. "Are there mirrors? Answer the damn question!"

A rapid and pleading answer came back. "No, no mirrors."

I opened the door and pulled it open and exhaled as I saw two men, although scared and confused, completely normal with no abnormal throat eyes, or eyes gouged out. "We have got to move quickly and get to the Armoury. We need weapons," I whispered as I started down the passageway. Mira stopped me.

"I don't think weapons will be the answer," the young man answered sheepishly.

I stopped and walked toward the young man. "Why? What do you think?"

Mira hesitated for a moment and then looked at the two of us. "When I was in the rack resting with the other lads before the ship started lunging around, I saw a few of the guys huddled around a mirror. All of them were just staring at it and then I saw an arm come through and pull them into the mirror one by one."

I stood straight and looked back at Mira. "I saw the same thing but keep going, maybe you know more."

Boats stared in disbelief at both of us and just shook

his head. "Yes, please continue, because I don't know what either of you is talking about."

Mira continued. "After the hand pulled the first two bloke's heads through the mirror, it pushed them back out except they both looked really different. One was missing his mouth, and the other had an extra eye, but both of them were just howling with laughter. The third guy was still holding the mirror, but he must have broken out of his trance for a second because he just sort of freaked out and then dropped the mirror on the deck. It shattered and then the other two guys just crumbled and fell to the ground. I watched the third guy check them out, but they did not move. He ran out of the room and I walked over to check on them and saw that both of their faces had returned to normal. That's when I ran and ended up coming in here. Before all hell broke loose."

Boats looked at me. "Sir, do you think any of this is tied to the anomaly we saw in the water up above? You know that strange green glow and coldness."

I stared down for a moment and spoke almost to myself. "Seems like it probably could be. Maybe we were drawn into that object and it served as some kind of portal. My only question is how do we get out of it?"

Boats only shook his head. "Not sure how we can steer the ship out of it, but it does seem like breaking the mirror might break a connection with the anomaly."

I nodded as Boats continued his hurried nervous talking. "I know it sounds crazy, but maybe we need to go through the ship and smash as many mirrors as we can find. It would make sense to start in the living quarters because that would stop the majority of the infected, right?"

"That's a good call, Boats. Let's start there and then go through each of the separate cabins."

We moved quickly down to the living spaces and stopped at the Armoury to add to my pistol and sword. I found a small pouch of gunpowder with matches and brought it along with extra bullets. We arrived at the crew's living quarters and found no one there, to our surprise.

"How are we going to find every mirror on the ship," Mira asked.

I shook my head slowly. "Does not matter, we just need to hope we get enough to be able to get rid of most of the infected. We will have to figure out the rest afterward."

With no better plan, he nodded and proceeded to shatter the one mirror in the living quarters. As the mirror cracked and shattered, we heard cries and screams come from above. I felt fear racing throughout my body as a shiver ran through me. We continued until the mirror was completely destroyed and then made our way to the forward part of the ship where a few regular cabins, including the Captain's, resided. Starting in the smaller cabins, we looked through each, only finding one mirror that we quickly smashed and destroyed. Mira found one additional mirror in one of the other cabins when we heard a commotion coming from my cabin.

I motioned for the other two men to get behind me as we moved in formation down the passageway to my cabin. Boats took station on the other side of the door and waited for me to give the order. I nodded and Boats opened the door with his pistol drawn and sword ready. As I entered, the Gunner's Mate burst out of the room knocking me back against the bulkhead, causing me to drop my pistol. I looked up and saw what used to be my friend, now only a distorted head covered by a rounded stem atop his neck with one large mouth that opened to show two rows of sharp teeth. The teeth chattered like someone stuck out in the snow from freezing temperatures.

Momentarily stunned, I sat against the bulkhead as the creature pounced toward me. Boats jumped into the creature just before it reached me and pulled it to the deck as they wrestled. I lunged for the pistol sitting three feet from me and turned to help Boats as I saw the two rows of teeth tear into the flesh on the side of his neck, ripping out the left side of his throat and letting loose a cry of delight as it stood over his body. I unloaded a single shot into the creature's head and watched as it ceased laughing and sat motionless in the pool of blood coming from the side of Boat's neck as he lay ghost white on the deck, dead.

I stood in shock with the empty pistol still locked in both hands, staring in horror at the man on the deck, when Mira touched the back of my arm. Flinching around, I pulled the weapon up as if to fire and then relaxed as I saw the young man near tears standing in front of me. "Sir, I just saw a group of them go into the Captain's cabin. We have to go, now!"

I snapped out of my trance and steadied. "Wait, no. We have to finish this and I think the Captain's stateroom is where the main entrance mirror must be."

We moved down the hallway and found the doorway open and crowded with several of the former crew—each with a different horrifying feature protruding from where their head used to reside. The Captain stood in front of the group with his familiar single large eye protruding from his throat. "Come in Mr Johnson, we have been expecting you."

Mira held my arm, trying to prevent me from entering the room, but I simply looked back with a confident and calm demeanour. "When I give you the signal, run out of here as fast as you can and take cover."

Mira gave me a confused look, but before he could say another word, I entered the room and confronted the Captain. I walked up to face him and just as the minion behind him started towards me I muttered. "Wait, I want to see. I came in to see, don't you understand. I want to see the other side."

The Captain motioned with a high-pitched shriek and the rest of the crew stopped and backed away as he walked slowly toward me. Two other creatures held my arms secure. Mira stood outside the doorway quietly and peered inside as the events unfolded.

Mira watched as the Captain's shriek changed and motioned toward the opposite side of the cabin. The rest of the crew of creatures parted, exposing a large mirror that looked like a pool of flowing black lava. I approached the mirror as the rest of the crew bit and snarled in approval and stopped directly in front of the reflection I recognised from earlier leaving my cabin.

I turned and caught Mira's surprised and confused gaze. "I am ready to see," I said slowly as I nodded in the direction of Mira, and then turned back to face the grinning reflection.

The hand stretched out towards me as I resisted the urge to fight back. I allowed it to grab my head, and I felt the tug pull me toward the mirror. As my head moved closer, I reached into the satchel I had hidden in my belt and lit the small pouch of gunpowder. As my head protruded through the mirror gateway, I could feel my mind being torn away. I extended my arm, poured the gunpowder into the mirror and closed my eyes.

Mira watched. The explosion ripped from inside the portal, the black lava liquid blowing back into the Captain's cabin. All of the creatures screamed in pain and collapsed to the deck. The Captain fell to his knees and let out a tremendous shriek that pierced the entire ship. Mira ran as fast as he could up as high as possible, trying to outrun the catastrophe below. A shudder shook through the ship and Mira fell from the ladder, hitting the deck hard. He tried to raise his head but as he fought to keep his eyes open, darkness enveloped him. He waited for death to find him before finally submitting to the darkness.

Mira awoke to sunlight reflecting off the top of the water as the waves brushed lightly off the sides of the ragged piece of wood floated innocently on the surface. He looked up, trying to guard his eyes from the intense sunlight as he noticed several men staring down at him from a small boat now tugging him inside. As the men pulled him roughly into the craft, he turned his head to see the enormous outline of the Expedition bearing down over the wreckage of his former pirate ship. Mira was escorted down into a dark space deep within the large galleon where the British commanders bound his hands and legs while he awaited interrogation. Mira drifted in and out of consciousness and each time stayed lucid for short amounts of time. A guard was stationed outside of the space and Mira listened carefully to his conversations with one of the medical staff tending to him. Mira looked around and squinted his eyes, trying to adjust his vision, and saw that he was strapped to the single rack in the room in addition to the chains around his arms and legs.

His wounds had been haphazardly bandaged. He suspected just enough to allow him to answer enough questions about his former crew and ship as well as any incriminating intelligence he could provide about his former Captain's intentions. He could hear the guard speaking to the medical attendant outside the room.

"I heard we are not getting underway for a while," the guard said to the attendant. "Something about a weird green layer they seemed to have found. They think that had something to do with what happened, but I guess this guy must have killed the whole crew or something. Dirty pirate scum. He doesn't look like much to me, but I was ordered to shoot to kill if anything happens."

The guard continued to brag as Mira shook his head and tried to free his arms. Confusion and remorse for his crew, especially Mr Johnson and Boats, flowed through him as he fought to suppress the terrible nightmarish memories.

The guard continued. "Think the Admiral has some questions for this guy, too. They are supposed to be aboard later today." The attendant acknowledged the man and went about gathering supplies for the next round of treatment for Mira.

Mira looked up at the ceiling and fought through his dismay, and then a new fear overcame him. Surely, we are not in the same area as the Ferocity, right next to the strange green portal. He worried that even though Mr Johnson blew up the portal, maybe there were still remnants of the evil left around. He tried to free his hands again and then gave up against the restraints. He heard movement outside the space and suspected it must be close to his interview with the British Navy. He wondered about how they would take his story as he tried to even believe it himself.

A noise came from behind him, sounding like a sharp crack of glass. He strained his neck and twisted his back to try and make out what formed the sound. As he twisted, he saw a small pail on the opposite side wall and, to his horror, a mirror hung above it. Gnarly fingers attached to a wrinkled hand extended out from the mirror and he screamed. The guard outside ignored the cries instead yelling back. "Shut up in there pirate scum, or I will give you something to scream about."

Mira yelled back. "You don't understand. They are coming back."

The guard laughed and continued ignoring the sounds from the room.

Meanwhile, in the isolated cabin, Mira felt the cold

fingers touch the top of his head and pull him and the rack toward the mirror.

On the other side of the black lava reflection, he could hear the familiar voice of Mr Johnson cry out, "Come join us, Mira. Everyone is welcome on the other side."

WHERE THE WIND DARES NOT

CLINT FOSTER

"Upon a night where wind doth hide and elsewhere sail the clouds,

All who sit upon the water should fear, soon, to drown,

Take a breath before comes death, or seek a blazing flame.

For doldrums damn the bravest men, whose fates are all the same."

The crew of the Robin clapped and whistled for their captain, who took an elegant leg and doffed his feathered cap. Almost invisible against the sea and sky behind him, his tawdry blue coat lay as flat as the sails. The doldrums had hit a day ago, and though they had oars, the Robin's crew were used to swift sailing on command of their seasoned captain. Breegan had rarely met with such staunch resistance by the skies, and though he kept his spirit lively, the drought of wind offered him pause. Legends told on the seas are many, but not all those legends are myths.

"Lady Redmane, fetch me a tankard of our finest grog and order Dierk to cook something with meat in it for dinner."

"I'm right here, sir." Dierk's heavy voice rumbled out of a shadow near the mast.

"Avast!" Breegan gasped. "A deserter! A sentence to double lashings and half rations for abandoning your post at the pot. If we can't tighten your belt with the whip, I don't know how we'll do it."

The crew roared with laughter at their captain's antics, dispersing to tend to their manifold duties aboard the Robin. Finch to scrub the cannons, though they gleamed with a greasy sheen already. Gorlin Crow to the nest, whereupon he might nap for a spell without catching the ire of his captain. Dom belowdecks to inspect the bilge. Ruckman to inventory their dwindling supply of ale. Skyler to keep an eye on Ruckman. Carrot to watch them both. And so on.

Stealing away into his cabin, Breegan absentmindedly browsed the maps pinned to the scarred walls. He spoke aloud, softly, to the ship, "Lady Robin, have thee mercy upon your captain. Steer me toward wind and waves once more." Just as he finished his prayer, Mate Gwyn kicked the door open and shuffled in with two sloshing mugs of grog. "I don't remember ordering a drink for you as well."

"I heard it clear as day." Stone faced and sharp. She never failed to draw a snort from Breegan. She sat on the desk, squinting at the map on the wall and musing, "I've never known you to be lost, nor short on gales in sails. No one I've ever met knows more of the magic of the sea than you, Breegan. Give me something to tell the crew I overheard."

It was not the first time her intuition hit the bullseye, and Breegan sighed at having made such a cunning mind his first mate. "You should've been a captain."

"I will be. I paid for this ship, after all. When yer tenure is up, I can put a feather in my hat just the same as ye."

He nodded, gulping from his mug, "A doldrums happens for a reason on Wesrin. That's what the Prae-stans say, anyway. When there's wind there's no worry. When there's no wind…"

"We could take to oars." Gwyn suggested. Breegan gave her a raised eyebrow, but she continued, "I know they'd bitch, but they'd rather that than swim."

"If we take to oars, we disturb the water." He said the words with a darkness Gwyn never knew him to feel, and his eyes were low and solemn. "Creatures in this sea gather to still waters, and not all tales are of fairies."

From above there came a double bell and the Crow in his nest, "Cap'n to the deck, hands at the rigging. Heavy clouds ahead, buccos."

Before Gwyn had a chance to reply, Breegan had slid around her, snatched his hat off the desk, and swept through the door with a cry, "Clouds mean storms, an' storms mean wind and waves, me bucco's. Safety lines on your waists and eyes open. It seems the salt has sent us our gale."

"Sir?" the crow's voice again called down, but it was shaky and almost impossible to hear. "That doesn't look like a cloud fer stormin'."

Turning east, Breegan could see a heavy mist rolling across the mirror-still ocean. In an instant, his demeanour changed. Gone was the confident smirk, the careless lilt of his head, the jovial tone in his voice. Serious as death, he roared, "All hands below deck on the hop. Lanterns and torches to the last and light up our Robin's belly from within."

The crew knew better than to ignore such an order, for seldom had they heard strain like it in their captain's voice. Even the crow veritably soared down from the nest, and only moments passed before Gwyn and Breegan stood alone at the wheel. The mist consumed the horizon, swarming toward them without so much as a breath of wind. Gone was the sun, smothered behind the wall of water turned air. "You too, Gwyn. I'll be down once I tie the helm straight."

She gave one long look at the fog and disappeared to join the crew below. Breegan took a length of rope and lashed it across the nearest rail, tying a sure knot to keep them from drifting. Taking up his own lantern from the sconce in his cabin, he stepped onto the deck just in time for the heavy air to roll over top of him.

Gone were the familiar sounds of heavy boots on deck, the shuffling of ropes, the rippling of the canvas in the wind. No water could be heard splashing across the prow of the Robin, and though Breegan called out to his crew to stay where they were, even that was muted by the thick air. His jacket soaked through and weighed heavily on his shoulders, and the hat dropped so low over his eyes he had to take it off just to see. His nostrils filled as though he was breathing water, and opening his mouth made him gulp and gasp. The fog smothered him, bearing him to the deck as his vision darkened on the edges. He tried to walk, and his boots slipped out from beneath him. Crawling with his hands, he could make no progress over the sudden slickness that afflicted the whole of the ship. Even when, to embolden himself if for nothing else, he tried to draw his sword from its sheath on his waist, so too did his hands slip from the handle, and he was left alone without even the sound of his own shallow breath on the damp wood and not so much as a weapon by way of comfort.

When he felt there was no more breath to draw, and his sight failed him, Breegan felt the deck begin to creak and sway. Then it began to tilt. Higher and higher the bow of the ship seemed to climb, as though trying to escape the mist by taking to the sky. Or as though it were lifted from the water by some nightmare force none of the crew had ever imagined. To Breegan, it mattered not how it seemed to tilt, but that he could not grasp a handhold, or a railing, or a board as the angle grew crazier by the moment until, at last, he began slipping backward toward the sea.

"Cap'n? Cap'n Breegan?" Gwyn's shaky voice carried over the still water.

"Mate Gwyn? Dare I ask if ye've a rope to carry me aboard?" Breegan was stretched flat on his back across a few wayward planks that had fallen overboard. How he managed to climb atop them he could not remember. With a deep, clean breath, he opened his eyes to see a clear sky. Cloudless and still, but clear.

After some hauling and swearing, Gwyn grabbed Breegan's sky coloured jacket by the collar and pulled him bodily on deck. They gasped together, laying on their backs as the sun so far above gently warmed and dried them. Finally, Breegan rolled over and tapped two fingers to an eyebrow in a mock salute, "Thanks, m'lady. I'd tip my cap to you, but I'm afraid the mist took more than my dignity."

"Took more than your hat, too." Gwyn's boots scuffed the deck as she walked. Her eyes lingered on a ruddy new stain on the deck. "Corrin had a home, a wife. She'll need to be told."

"Aye. We'll tell her." Sitting cross-legged, Breegan passed his eyes over the ship. Corrin was face down on the deck, a cold, wet torch stick in his hand. "Could you hear anything?"

Gwyn shook her head.

"For the best. And the crew?

"Below decks, awaitin' orders."

"A good crew."

"A nervous crew." Gwyn cast him a glance that said more than her words, and he nodded. He noticed his hat stuck against the railing and stooped to gather it, donning the sopping tricorn and adopting the closest thing to his customary grin as he could manage.

Whenever sailors spoke of the Mist, it was with reverence and respect, as though it were a thing to be treated with dignity so as to avoid it. "This mist is a thing beyond mortals, Gwyn. It is the reclaiming spirits of the restless, the unjust souls that met ill fates upon the waves." He shook his head slowly, "Order all hands armed with at least one shot." The look he gave her was more dreadful than any sight she'd seen. "Anything so as not to die without air in our lungs, drowned without even tasting the salt of the sea." He shuddered. They were grateful for the ordinary sounds of the ship, even as still as it was, groaning and echoing hollowly.

They were quiet for some time as the captain inspected his ship. Even if they took to oars, the crew could scarcely propel the Robin as fast as the Mist had overtaken them. And if they did outrun the Mist, there would likely be other things to deal with. Things with more teeth and less irony. Breegan pieced it together, "We're stranded."

"Aye."

"As first mate, I expect you to address me as, 'Captain.'"

Gwyn made a point not to give him the satisfaction of a reply or even a glare.

"Insubordination is punishable by lashing. Seeing as we're down a bosun, I'll administer them myself, but shall take no pleasure in the act-"

"The lashings of yer tongue in yer cheeks are enough punishment for me. As for the jokes, I see no reason for levity given our current company and predicament."

"In the face of such horror, we can naught but laugh

away the heaviness of our thoughts or succumb to them."

She growled, "I can think of something else you can succumb to."

"That's the spirit." Gaining his feet, he traveled the length and breadth of the Robin. As was tradition for sailors who die on Wesrin, he flicked two heavy golden coins over the rail with his thumb. "One coin for your service, one for a drink. Hail the fallen, and let the salt be satisfied."

They shared a silent nod before Gwyn hefted the door to the hold ajar and introduced the captain back to his crew.

"We thought you was lost, Cap'n."

"Overboard in the Mist, eh? Salted for certain."

"Cap'n of the Robin won't be had by no weather."

"Breegan, the Sire of Salt himself, back from the dead."

Whispers and cheers greeted him alike, as they often had. His grin need only be feigned for a moment. Another successful avoidance of certain death was but another notch in his legacy. That tale had grown long indeed, and though the Mist offered him far more worry than he let on. The instant his boot-heel tapped the dampened hold of the ship, his swagger emerged tenfold as strong as it had been. "Aye, ye dogs!" His voice filled the ship with fire, "Gaze upon yer captain and know that no such weather shall belay my presence from my crew. Overboard? Lost at sea? These are but trifles to the Sire of Salt himself, and I bid ye chastise yerselve's fer doubtin'."

Their chuckles, nervous as they were, reassured

him, and he set about divvying responsibilities for the day and preparations for the night.

Over the course of the afternoon, they had no worries of weather, and the horizon on all sides proved stable and still. Breegan ordered a rest to work come sunset, and the crew drank freely from the barrels in the belly of the Robin.

Come evening, Crow alone remained uninebriated and above decks, gazing with intent in all directions with his eyes that never quite settled each upon the same object. A sliver of moon shone wanly behind a smattering of inkblot clouds, and though her light was bright, it was often hidden. Striving as he might against the spotty darkness, Crow was at ease, high in the nest. Above the deck, apart from the crew, he felt somehow fulfilled, and loved the sensation of gut-wrenching vertigo that often greeted him when he stood and gazed brazenly down the rigging to the deck. Yet, even as he gazed to the east and saw but glass sea and slow-rolling clouds overhead, there came from the west, borne upon a soundless gale of dread and doom, a dense, drowning fog.

Had he gazed west, perhaps he might have spotted the mist as it rolled so ominously onward over the mirror sea. Had he gazed west, perhaps it may have come from the east, and was, in the end, fated to come upon the Robin unnoticed, compass be damned. None can say but those who wonder at the maybes of the past, and there were only sureties aboard the Robin that night. Darkness like hell overcame the crew, and they choked and sputtered even as they strove to breathe the heavy air. No warning had they, and their voices carried not even so much as inches from their cloying throats as they cried in hopes of saving others with their final breaths. Bad luck or worse, fate saw a half dozen of the crew making their rounds, drunken and stumbling, even as the Mist bore down upon the Robin. These had no lanterns and did their work by the light of the silver moon.

Then it was dark, and the mist filled their nostrils and throats. Boots already tottering slipped and splayed men across the deck. What few could manage to draw their blades in time chose to bury the steel at their hips within their breasts than to die the worst death a sailor could die. Better to meet a swift end at the point of steel than a slow, breathless, choking end.

Breegan was in his cabin with Gwyn, both several mugs deep and a pipe and half between them. He was telling her a story about his most recent run-ins with the Praestans when suddenly his words came out as a gasp, and they fell dead on the very air. Gwyn, only an arm away, was gone, and the half-white droplets of air laden with water glazed his sight. Dampness overtook his heavy blue coat, and again his hat sank low over his eyes. It was foolish to shout, but he did so nonetheless. Even as the rational part of his brain protested against his fearful screams, his body revolted against the reality it now faced, and he cried into the heavy air of fate. He would have done better to have stayed silent.

Gwyn, more disciplined, more defiant, more restrained, held her breath fast against the Mist as it swirled around her face, oozing into her open eyes and choking out her very pores. She thought she saw Breegan's shadow howling in the near distance, obscured by the thick, cloying air, but could not be certain. She would have felt better had she screamed.

Heat.
Light.
Voices.
Breath.
Breegan's gasp tore his throat bloody and raw as the torch banished the Mist in his cabin. Nearly as bright as the flames, Gwyn's crimson hair blazed above him as she gave him a cluck with her tongue, "Dying isn't as hard as you seem to make it."

"You know," he grunted as she heaved him to his feet, nodding his thanks as she plopped the drenched hat on his head nearly a full turn left wise of right. "I've never met anyone what survived the Mist. And we've done it twice.

"We've many miles between us and land, and the Mist rules every inch of it." She sat wearily on the deck, propping her chipped and scarred sword up by the hilt. In a moment, her head was leaned forward, and she was snoring gently.

"Aye. Rest, lady. A still sea with flat sails and naught but salty rats for company, I imagine ye've done precious little enough of that."

Gwyn slept, the torch falling from her hand into Breegan's, and the Mist rolled away from the Robin. Breegan took stock of their supplies and did his best to judge how far the coast was back to the east. He had been sailing longer than most who still wore the feather in their cap and called themself captain, but he was never too proud to rely on his instruments and subordinates. Now, in a distinct shortage of one and fearing to wake the other, he felt a loneliness that was made all the worse by the presence of Crow's body, a broken, sodden pile bleeding on the deck. Breegan hoped it was the fall that killed him.

Breegan spent most of the sunless morning gazing out to the east, squinting for any sign of sand or sail. Or Mist.

"Weather thee the wind and waves until the sea is still,

And weather next that which perplexes even as it kills.

Care, take thee, to breathe before and not the Mist, inhale,

Lest, like those still winds and waves, thy falleth flat as sails."

With a gentle prod from her boot, Gwyn shook Breegan awake. He had been mumbling for some time, and though most of it was unintelligible, what made sense made enough sense for her to wake him. He snorted and bolted upright, unconsciously wiping the drool from the corner of his mouth and already speaking, "Mate Gwyn to the fore decks and aweigh the anchor, sails t' th' winds an' weather."

She shushed him with a mug. And they enjoyed the sunrise together, sharing a pipe between them while Bol's eye rose over the horizon. They set the crew to work offering gold to the Salt and burying their comrades in the great blue tomb that had room aplenty. Their numbers were dwindling, and Breegan could not quench the voice in his mind that spoke unbidden.

Less crew means more food.

The strong survive.

Should we save the bodies?

Breegan knew what hunger was. He hoped those who remained need not stray unto those treacherous waters where men wade in times of a crisis of the stomach. Fish and stale bread was better than the alternative. Breegan knew what hunger was.

Two weeks of windless, glassy sea. Fish flitted just out of reach of their nets, taunting the sailors with their shimmering scales, flashing, tantalising lights as dazzling as angels. As damnable as the devil. The fish ate heartily of the dead.

The voice in Breegan's mind spoke, louder with each passing day, so could we.

The bread was gone. No crumbs even fit for licking off the deck. Not anymore. The ale barrels were dry. Not even sticky with residue, but crackling, maddeningly dry. They had not even the scent of beer upon them any longer. What remained of the water was bracken and stale. Another few such sunrises would see fighting. The crew's eyes narrowed. They grew hunted, haunted looks. The imaginations of their fellows and friends hated the idea of a time when they might kill a man for his meat but knew that time was drawing nigh.

And then a call from the new crow in his nest, "Mist off the starboard side!"

It was upon them.

Their torches burned hot and bright, banishing the cloying waters of the air in a small bubble around the safety of their blaze. Huddled together, shivering, hungry, and afraid, the crew looked to Breegan. His endless optimism, his unbridled love for the sea, his carefree, almost jaunty treatment of threats in the past made his stony silence of the present all the harder to bear.

Afore decks, one of the torches spluttered, and coughed, and sizzled out.

When the sun finally broke through, the drowned bodies of the dead crewmates were not tossed overboard.

Breegan guessed it had bought them another week.

And after that week?

He grit his teeth against the thought.

Thrice more did the Mist wash over the Robin and drench the crew. They knew now that torches were their only shelter. A few had gone belowdecks in the hope of staying safe, but these were found face down in the bilge. It was like as not they drowned in the scummy, wretched bile there in the bowels of the ship. Whenever the oppressive, wet air swept through them, it extracted a grisly toll, and their supply of oil and torch rags was not endless.

Rather than attempt a mutiny, for what good could

come of such treachery now, several of the crew took to the barq lashed to the Robin's port side. They dropped to the glassy water in spite of Breegan's warnings, laying off with oars and gaunt, haggard glances at the sapphire sea. Not even a hundred yards from the Robin, Breegan could already see the first of dozens of monsters that took a turn haranguing and hunting the barq. In less than an hour, the small boat was splinters, sinking soundlessly. The crewmates were shreds of ragged flesh and dirty cloth, and the survivors aboard the Robin could find no solace from their horrid screams as betentacled, toothed, and clawed monsters ravaged them from below. Soon enough, all was still, the only evidence of their failed escape the cloudy red patch on the horizon to port.

***

The last of the crew, the cook, Dierk, looked from Gwyn to Breegan and back. "Cap'n," he nodded at Gwyn, "Mate Gwyn." He licked his crusted lips, eyes flitting and bloodshot, "Permission to end my service, sir?" When he looked up, Breegan could see his lower lip quiver and the tears welling behind his eyes. The picked-over skeletons of the rest of the crew grinned at them, mocking the living with their peaceful silence and stares.

A forgotten, shadowy part of Breegan's mind quipped, But Dierk, if you die, who will cook us dinner?

The bolder part of it, the voice Breegan had first feared, then hated, and begrudgingly fallen under the control of, retorted, the cook for dinner. The cook for dinner. The cook for dinner.

Gwyn's pleading eyes bore into Breegan's skull.

But he could not bear to turn and look at her.

"Aye, crewman Dierk. You have my permission, and my apology."

Somehow, Dierk managed a wry grin, "Doldrums ain't no cap'n's carelessness, sir. Just shit luck." The grin did not last long as he glanced again toward the prow of the ship where the crew gazed outward at them accusingly.

Gwyn made a small noise in her throat as the cook drew a knife from a sling on his back. With a stern nod, he looked toward the last of the crew who had sustained him yet this long and pulled the edge of the dagger across his throat. His blood mingled with theirs. Neither Breegan nor Gwyn had the heart to slide him overboard.

A few hours passed as they stared into the growing slick of blood beneath Dierk's body.

Finally, when the sun was low over their shoulders, not that it lessened the stifling, unstirring heat, Gwyn's hooded eyes passed over to her captain. Tears without the water to fall shone in her eyes and a withering hand rose in front of her face, pointing west. "When it comes again, what do we do?"

"Die, probably." He did not turn to look at her. To do so would have betrayed his own fears. "Don't look at me like that."

She might, but you'll waste and rot.

The Robin will sink you to the depths, a thing of bones and white, wrinkled flesh glued to the sands while it drowns forever.

She ground her teeth.

Eternity awaits.

It was a damned way to die, Breegan felt. Almost any other path to the end would be preferable than drowning without even the taste of the salt on one's lips or starving to death while the teeming ocean mocked you from below. Better to die by the sword. By flames. By anything.

It came without the clamour of battle, without the thundering doom of a storm o'erhead, without heat or pain. There was the moon, that bravest of crows, standing watch in the highest nest of them all. Then there was darkness. Breegan roared into the Mist like a blade of grass against the falling snow. Gwyn screamed in defiance. She may as well have whispered.

The deck buckled from the creeping, infusing wetness that sent the mighty boughs and boards of the Robin crackling to tinder. Breegan bellowed until the air left his lungs and the world fell, dark and damp. He felt the deck rise up to slam into his face. He felt the wet air press down on his chest so that when he tried again to breathe; he found he could only writhe. He tried to swallow a gulp of air, but it clung, thick and hot, inside his throat.

Darkness overtook him.

But a whisper haunted his dream. "Kill me."

The sword was heavy on his belt, glued to the deck under the weight of the wet air. He could not tell if his eyes were open but felt Gwyn's breath on his side.

"Captain. Please."

Her words were thick and gurgly, as though she spoke through a bowl of jelly. A cough. Then she retched, the last of her air leaving her in a strangled heave. His blade would not slide from the sheath, and she fell with a dull, distant thud, her face twisted in fear and horror as her captain failed her.

Then there was silence.

The Mist clung to him, dragged him to the deck until the soft, damp wood formed to the bones of his face. Moisture condensed on his lips and smothered his senses. There was only darkness. Only wet. Only the Mist. It reached into his throat and dripped viscous limbs into his chest, filling him with water until it ran from his eyes and nose in streams. Yet still he lived.

The blood in his veins ran blue, then white, then clear, and he sunk to the depths with the Robin. A thing of water claimed by the Mist.

Dawn broke and banished the Mist, but too late by far for the Robin and her captain. The death-still sea bent, rippled, and pulsed with the first few breaths of wind in months. Bulging canvas brought new, unwary ships and sailors into the path of the doldrums anew, and the Mist clung hungrily to dark, laden clouds, waiting for a still sea and desperate crews.

None heard again of the red-haired mate, nor the blue-clad Captain Breegan, though his legends live on in his stead. The ports and inns from Korm to Pelenar have since found many a coin given for stories of the Robin and her doomed crew. The Mist, and the fear of it, give weight to many a story weaver's pouch on Wesrin's coast. The more superstitious crews offer prayers to Breegan, Captain of the Salted. Others remember Gwyn for keeping her captain's company to the end. Few dare scoff or doubt the tale of the Mist and the Robin. Though sailors choose with abandon which of their songs and myths to treat like truths, many still sing in earnest of the Robin for fear of the Mist where the wind dares not.

ABOUT THE AUTHORS

DAVID GREEN is a writer based in Co Galway, Ireland. Growing up between there and Manchester, UK meant David rarely saw sunlight in his childhood, which has no doubt had an effect on his dark writings. Published with Black Ink Fiction, Red Cape Publishing and Eerie River Publishing, David has been nominated for the Pushcart Prize 2020 and his dark fantasy series Empire of Ruin launches in June 2021 with "In Solitude's Shadow."

Website: www.davidgreenwriter.com
Newsletter: https://tinyurl.com/y6ah8brp
Twitter: @davidgreenwrite

TIM MENDEES is a horror writer from Macclesfield in the North-West of England that specialises in cosmic horror and weird fiction. A lifelong fan of classic weird tales, Tim set out to bring the pulp horror of yesteryear into the 21st Century and give it a distinctly British flavour. His work has been described as the lovechild of H.P. Lovecraft and P.G. Wodehouse and is often peppered with a wry sense of humour that acts as a counterpoint to the unnerving, and often disturbing, narratives.

Tim has had over seventy published stories in anthologies and magazines with publishers all over the world. His novellas, Burning Reflection, Spiffing, and The Creeping Void are out now.

When he is not arguing with the spellchecker, Tim is a goth DJ, crustacean and cephalopod enthusiast, and the presenter of a popular web series of live video readings of his material and interviews with fellow authors. He currently lives in Brighton & Hove with his pet crab, Gerald, and an army of stuffed octopods.

https://timmendeeswriter.wordpress.com/
https://tinyurl.com/timmendeesyoutube

C. MARRY HULTMAN is an American genre fiction writer, teacher and literary scholar who currently resides and works in Sweden. He has had several stories published in various anthologies, won the Racine Public Library Writing Challenge and hosts the podcast The Guild. His supernatural noir novel Face of Fear was published in 2020 and is still available wherever books are sold.

He lives with his wife, two daughters and the cat Fizzgig.

https://linktr.ee/C.MarryHultman

ERIC LABRIE GILES is a former Canadian musician and music composer who diverted into writing some years ago. He specializes mainly in dark stories, science-fiction, dystopian, weird, cosmic, and horror stuff. Algernon Blackwood, Ray Bradbury, and Frank Belknap Long stand among his favorite authors, alongside H.P. Lovecraft, Ambrose Bierce and so many others. From 2019 to 2021, Eric has seen over forty of his works published, either as part of themed anthologies or as stand-alone. Eric has also self-published two dystopian novels and a horror novelette.

PETER J. FOOTE is a bestselling speculative fiction writer from Nova Scotia, Canada. Most of his stories are within the genres of Science Fiction, Fantasy, and Horror.

Outside of writing, he runs a used bookstore specializing in fantasy & sci-fi, cosplays with his wife, and alternates between red wine and coffee as the mood demands.

Believing that an author should write what he knows, many of Peter's stories reflect his personal life and experiences.

As the founder of the group "Genre Writers of Atlantic Canada", Peter believes that the writing community is stronger when it works together.

You can find Peter on:

Facebook Twitter Newsletter.

www.facebook.com/peterjfooteauthor/

https://twitter.com/PeterJFoote1

https://www.subscribepage.com/c3j4h4

G. ALLEN WILBANKS is a writer living in Northern California, where he writes horror and fantasy fiction in a desperate attempt to quiet the voices in his head. He is a member of the Horror Writers Association (HWA) and has published over 200 short stories in Daily Science Fiction, Deep Magic, and many other magazines and online venues. His work has also appeared in several internationally best-selling anthologies.

G. Allen has released two short story collections and several novels. His most recent book, Testing Grounds, came out in July, 2021. For more information you can visit his website at www.gallenwilbanks.com.

JONATHAN INBODY is an author, filmmaker, and podcaster from Buffalo, New York. He specializes in writing horror and science fiction, but also writes any other genre that can have a monster in it. He is an avid reader of early 20th century Weird Fiction and an aficionado of B-movie genre cinema, and his acid horror anthology podcast Gray Matter, which combines his love of both, is coming soon.

Twitter: https://twitter.com/InbodyWriter

DALE PARNELL lives in Staffordshire, England, with his wife and their imaginary dog, Moriarty. He writes fiction, mainly fantasy, science-fiction and horror, along with the occasional poem. He has self-published two collections of short stories and a poetry collection to date and is featured in over thirty excellent anthologies.

You can find Dale on Facebook and Instagram as @ shortfictionauthor

MARK RANKIN

Based in West Yorkshire, England, Mark is a writer who loves exploring the supernatural.

His debut novel The Heart That Died now out for query, he writes a personal blog and frequents several online writers' groups when not being really, really bad at video games.

Mark is a full-time wheelchair user on a mainly successful mission not to run over his cats.

SIMONE OLDMAN GREEN (they/them) is a genre-fluid writer and editor living in the Kingdom of Fife with husband, John. Author of over 70 published works with imprints including Dragon Soul Press, Black Hare Press and Eerie River Publishing. They also won 3rd Place in the British Fantasy Society's Short Story Contest 2018. Writer, vegan, martial artist, gamer, occasionally a terrible person (but only to fictional people). They thrive on the unusual, which might explain why there are so many cats. Website: https://thebasementoflove.blogspot.com/
Facebook:https://www.facebook.com/thebasementoflove
Twitter: https://twitter.com/SOGreenWriter

STEPHEN JOHNSON is a retired Naval Officer serving 22 years on four different ships over his career. He has published "The Hollow" in Eleanor Merry's Dark Halloween Holiday Flash Fiction Anthology and "The Other Side of the Mirror" in Scare Street's Night Terrors Volume 8.

CLINT FOSTER has published dozens of stories from poetry to horror and anything in between. He loves taking on new challenges and always hope someone enjoys his work. He lives in southern Iowa with his wonderful wife, Nik, and their herd of four legged children.

www.facebook.com/clintfosterauthor

**MORE FROM
BREAKING RULES
PUBLISHING EUROPE**

Face of Fear by C. Marry Hultman
e-book:books2read.com/u/49lVg0
Paperback: mybook.to/Face-of-Fear

Dawson Junior G3 by Brian Wagstaff
e-book:books2read.com/u/4EP99E
Paperback: mybook.to/Dawson

Boy in the Wardrobe by Esther Jacoby
e-book: mybook.to/Boy-Wardrobe

New Life Cottage by Esther Jacoby
e-book:books2read.com/u/m0wAzW
Paperback: mybook.to/New-Life-Cottage

The Wait by Esther Jacoby
e-book:https://books2read.com/u/4Dgz8Q

Liebe ist Warten by Esther Jacoby
e-book:https://books2read.com/u/mZaVD2
Paperback: mybook.to/Liebe

Musing on Death & Dying by Esther Jacoby
e-book:books2read.com/u/49lVg0
Paperback: mybook.to/Musings

Earth Door by Cye Thomas
e-book:books2read.com/u/mKyXKv
Paperback: mybook.to/Earth-Door

Graffiti Stories by Nick Gerrard
e-book:books2read.com/u/m2MQOR
Paperback: mybook.to/Grafitti-Stories

Punk Novelette by Nick Gerrard
e-book:books2read.com/u/4jLpqv
Paperback: mybook.to/Punk-Novelette

Struggle and Strife by Nick Gerrard
e-book:books2read.com/u/4DRyqr
Paperback: mybook.to/struggle-strife

Fake Escape by Natalie Hughes
e-book:https://books2read.com/u/bMXL5X

Murder Planet by Adam Carpenter
e-book:books2read.com/u/bMXllV
Paperback: mybook.to/Murder-Planet

Generation Ship by Adam Carpenter
e-book:books2read.com/u/49Nk8M
Paperback: mybook.to/generation

Cold as Hell by Neen Cohen
e-book:https://books2read.com/u/bxennv
Paperback: mybook.to/Grafitti-Stories

Six Days to Hell by E.L. Giles
e-book:https://books2read.com/u/bWrLyq
Paperback: mybook.to/SixDaystoHell

Just 13 anthology
e-book: https://books2read.com/u/mKy1B9

Lost Lore & Legends Anthology
e-book: books2read.com/u/m2RrwG
Paperback: mybook.to/Lost-Lore-Legends-pbk

Adventure Awaits volume 1 Anthology
e-book: https://books2read.com/u/3Gw8o8
Paperback : mybook.to/adventure_awaits_1

Death House
e-book: https://books2read.com/u/bWrODW
Paperback : mybook.to/deathhouse

Find us at:
www.breakingrulespublishingeuro.com

www.ingramcontent.com/pod-product-compliance
Lightning Source LLC
LaVergne TN
LVHW040001200726
843493LV00005B/1091